EXECUTING JUSTICE

JUSTICE

Concrete, Crooks and Blood

EXECUTING JUSTICE

Concrete, Crooks and Blood

Chris Beasley

Dedicated to:
DEONA

You truly are EPIC!

CONTENTS

CHAPTER 1

Getting Juan's Attention

"Man, you better call Alex. He's getting mad because he can't get you on the phone. Did you turn your phone off or somethin'?" asked Mike.

Juan began to pat his various pockets, searching for his phone. No success. In a few moments, he realized that he'd left it in his work truck. He jogged over and reached through the open window for his phone in the front seat. As he reached, he noticed that he still had dried concrete on his hands. He stopped and rubbed his hands together. Most of the grey, dusty mess crumbled off easily. Once satisfied that they were mostly clean, he did a final wipe on his jeans leaving dull, grey handprints against the blue denim. He reached for his phone and looked at his missed calls.

"Five missed calls," he mumbled to himself. "Three from Alex and two from DD."

Hitting the speed dial labeled 'Alejandro,' he got a swift answer.

"Hey, Juan. Where've you been, man?"

"I've been on this convenience store job all day. We got most of the slab poured."

"What do you mean, most?"

"We needed to do some rebar work the contractor didn't tell us about."

"That sucks. I thought you guys would've been done hours ago," Alex said, half accusing and half trying to be understanding. He really needed Juan at another site. They were getting behind and things weren't going as quickly as he had hoped. Deadlines were looming.

"We won't be finished today. There's still one more section we need to pour after we get it prepped," Juan said, looking at his watch. It was after five already. He was tired, dusty and sweaty.

Alex continued, "I needed you guys to go to the other loc..."

Bam!

There was a jolt to Juan's entire body as something violently crashed into his back. He lurched forward in pain. He tried to gain his balance, but his legs felt like tiny brittle match sticks. His phone tumbled to the ground with a hard *crack*. From Alex's end, all that he heard was an unusual *thunk* followed by a *click*.

"Hello! Hello!" The line was dead. "Humph... I wonder what that was all about?"

Juan was staggering and spun around just in time to glimpse a pipe slamming into his face. In vain, he tried to raise his arms in defense, but it was too late.

Crack!

His head snapped to the right, and he crumpled to the hard ground. Everything went black. Moments later, he realized he was on his back, and dark shadows were surrounding him. They felt rough and were pulling him, grabbing him. Confusion and terror reigned in his mind. Slowly, he started to gain clarity.

"Get off me!" he screamed with all the ferocity he could muster. With each terrifying moment the figures could be seen more clearly. They lifted him to his feet as he tried to fight back. He planted his feet to get leverage for his counterattack, but his knees failed him. As his body gave way, he knew he was in trouble. He staggered, held up by two men he'd never seen before. Regaining his senses, he glanced around, desperately hoping to see his crew. Then he remembered Mike, Joe and Jerry had driven off just after Mike told him to call Alex. He was alone and outmatched. The sense of helplessness warred against his courage.

One of the men snatched his hair and jerked up his head. His left eye and cheek were already red and starting to swell. He tasted the distinct flavor of blood, and, for the first time, he realized some of his teeth on the left side were loose. He expelled the blood that was rapidly filling his mouth by spitting, gagging and hacking. Inches from his face stood a well-dressed man. He seemed educated and business-like, as well as fierce and determined.

He eyed Juan and asked, "Mr. Fuente?"

"What the hell are you doing?" Juan answered angrily.

"Are you Juan Marc Fuente?" the man demanded.

"Who the hell are you?"

"Mr. Fuente, you're my tool to get your boss's attention. This will let him know how serious we are. Tell Alex to expect the message soon."

With that, the man Juan had come to think of as an angry accountant nodded to his two assailants. They threw him to the ground, and everything went dark.

When asked later about the situation, he never could say how long he was out.

The side of his face was the first thing he remembered feeling as he awoke. The pain had turned to throbbing. He was coming around when he heard an unfamiliar voice.

"Hey, buddy, you ok?"

Fear was his first reaction, and he pulled away with a jerk. He tried to stand up, but, like before, he couldn't seem to get his feet underneath him. He tried to get up a second time, but he felt a warm and friendly hand on his back.

"Sit down, buddy. Are you ok?"

Juan could barely process the question. He gazed up at a large, bald, black man. His frame shaded him from the setting sun, creating a massive silhouette. His face was gentle, concerned and questioning.

"You need me to call an ambulance, man?"

"No, no ambulance. I... I think I'm ok."

He was thinking that if he went to the hospital, they would have to notify the cops. That's more scrutiny than he wanted. He made a gesture to the man by holding up both hands.

"I'm alright, really. Just give me a minute."

"Mister, I'm gonna sit with you for a while. I'm still worried about you."

Juan Marc laid back and closed his eyes. Relaxing seemed to ease the pain. Somehow, he knew this man wouldn't let anything happen to him. Feeling exhausted, but safe, he surrendered to sleep.

CHAPTER 2

Finding Juan

Alex's frustration was mounting. He still hadn't heard from Juan and he was angry that his projects weren't moving forward fast enough. It had been late afternoon when Alex and Juan talked, and he assumed that he and Juan had simply been cut off. Now, his angst was growing because he still couldn't get his calls to go through. Exasperated, he cursed the cell phone carrier under his breath. Not until DD called him at home did he start to suspect something other than a technology problem.

"Alejandro?"

"Speaking."

"It's DD. Have you heard from Juan?"

Alex had assumed that his childhood friend and DD had been sleeping with each other. They never told him, but they discretely let it be known through casual conversation that they were seeing each other outside work. It wasn't long before Alex had put two and two together and realized they had been an item for quite some time. He knew the relationship had turned more intense in recent weeks. It was no wonder DD sounded rattled.

"Not recently. Earlier this afternoon, we were talking, and we got cut off. That was a couple of hours ago. I didn't think much of it at the time."

Now the cogs in Alex's mind were churning as well. Was it an ordinary dropped call or was something else going on?

"He was supposed to come to my place after work. I've called several times, but I can't get him to pick up," DD explained.

DD was a pro. She worked for Alex in his office handling payroll, scheduling and accounting. She had the uncanny ability to track down any wayward employee because she was a ninja on the phone. Her title of Office Manager had recently been elevated to Office Administrator. DD held his professional world together. Beyond that, she was also a trusted confidante. If she was concerned, there was a reason.

"Did you call his crew?"

"I got through to Mike and Joe. Joe says the last time he saw Juan, they were in a pickup at the site getting ready to leave. He said Mike got a call from you asking where Juan was. Mike got out of the truck and walked over to Juan, presumably to let him know you called. After that, Mike jumped back in the truck, and Jerry drove everyone home."

"Joe's story lines up. What did Mike say?"

"Mike said basically the same thing. He said Juan had left his phone in his truck and that he was headed for the truck to call you when the crew rolled out."

"Ok, well... that makes sense. The first place we need to check is the job site."

"What about his place? It's late. Why would he still be at the site?"

"You said it yourself. He wasn't supposed to go home. He was supposed to be with you."

"Good point. I'll meet you there." In seconds, she was out the door headed to the unfinished convenience store in her SUV.

* * *

"You think this is the end of the attack, rather it is only the beginning. Like a foul stench that comes on the wind, there is an approaching battle for the heart of our city. It will require a bloody and violent struggle between good and evil. The people you love will be raised up and called to fight on behalf of justice."

Juan was just beginning to stir and was trying to follow what his new friend just said. The man seemed to be talking nonsense. Still dazed, Juan knew he was sincere by the passion in his eyes and the iron firmness in his voice.

"Wait. What?"

"Remember my words."

"What are you talking about? Why is all of this happening?

"Because justice demands blood."

"I don't understand."

"I must go. Someone is coming to help you."
Juan assumed the man had called an ambulance. His face melted into a look of dread.

"Don't worry. It's not the ambulance or the police." A sigh escaped his mouth as he slumped back in relief. He watched reverently as the man silently crossed the street and disappeared.

In that moment, he recognized a familiar vehicle. A white Chevy Yukon pulled into the undeveloped parking lot. It was DD, and a wave of hope enveloped him. He pulled himself up, standing to meet her. The vehicle came to an abrupt stop as she jumped out and ran to him. She threw her arms around him, buried her head in his chest and tears welled up as she took in his familiar scent. They both savored the moment, their hearts grateful for the reunion. Sniffling, she released her embrace and stepped back to get a better look at him. The red welp across his face was glaring, and blood dripped in a dirty, crimson ooze from the corner of his mouth.

"What happened!?"

He thought for a moment, shaking his head. "I don't know. I was talking to Alex, and it felt like a sledgehammer hit me in the back." With his last remark, she stepped behind him and lifted his shirt. She saw a large red mark between his shoulders. Bruising was already starting to cause deep purple, black and blue stains under his skin. She gasped and her face grimaced.

"What!? Who did this to you?" she demanded over his shoulder.

"I told you, I don't know. They said something about a message." He turned towards her as he began touching the left side of his face gingerly, trying to assess where it hurt most. The most painful places were just above his eye, cheekbone and lower jaw. He pushed at his teeth with his tongue and then, from the outside, against his cheek with his fingers. No longer firmly in place, they squished back and forth in his gums as he probed them. He confirmed that two or three were loose.

"What message?" Her question brought his mind snapping back to the conversation.

"I don't know. He said to expect a message. He made it sound like it would come later or something." He started to think about the pain again. The pain in his back was starting to compete with the agony in his face. He raised his arms and rolled his shoulders back a few times, testing his range of motion and hoping to find a less tender way to carry himself. He cringed as he drew his shoulders back.

Another pair of headlights were pulling onto the lot. As the vehicle drove under the lamp post, they could both make out the distinctive shape of Alejandro's work truck. The "Just Plain Rocks" logo was on the side of the door. He brought the truck to a standstill, jumped out and ran over to the couple.

"What happened?" he said, looking at his friend's face. Before he heard the answer, he had already gathered that his friend had been beaten. He'd seen things like this before and he knew that this was no work injury.

"Not sure. Some guys jumped me. They told me that they had a message for you." He examined Alex's face, hoping he had some answers.

Alex, sensing that he was wanting information, replied, "Juan, I don't know of anyone that would do this. Sure, I've had a few bar fights. Maybe it's someone I've scrapped with?" But they both knew he was grasping at straws.

"Nah, I don't think so. This guy wouldn't be in your kind of bar."

"Whadaya mean?"

Juan began to describe the ordeal from the beginning. He described the initial blow to his back and two thugs holding him up while the man in the suit ran the show. The angry accountant had done all the talking. He described being thrown to the ground and abandoned. Then, his tone shifted completely when he told about the mysterious man who had come to his aid. He was grateful, although he had no idea how long the man had been there watching over him. Juan then tried in vain to remember what the man told him. It was important but it seemed elusive. The words were on the tip of his brain. Frustratingly, no matter how hard he tried to recall the message, he couldn't bring the words to the surface enough to repeat them. As he finished his story, he was starting to feel almost human.

"Let's get you to a doctor and call the cops," stated DD.

"Are you nuts?" said Alex.

"Why, what do you mean?" she said, taken aback at his tone. Then she realized that neither Alex nor Juan wanted to go to the hospital.

"The cops never help people like us. We don't even know the names of the guys who did this. We don't have a car description or anything for them to go on. They probably won't even believe his story," said Alex. "No offense, bro."

"None taken," Juan replied. "DD, it probably won't go anywhere. I don't know who they were. And whether or not I go to the hospital, I'll eventually heal up. I don't think anything is broken except some loose teeth and maybe my cheekbone.

Defiantly, she glared at them both. "Your cheekbone is my favorite part of your handsome face. If it wasn't for that left cheek, you and I wouldn't be together!" She started to crack a smile, and they realized she had lightened up. This was her weak attempt at a joke to cut through the seriousness of the moment. At first, they were both unsure where she was taking this, but when they saw her demeanor shift, they relaxed, smiled and let out an obligatory chuckle as well. She grabbed his shirt and gently pulled him close.

"You're gonna come to my place tonight. I'm gonna put some ice on those sore spots, get you a glass of wine and make you forget all about your little boo boos." Her tone had maintained its playful lilt. Juan recognized the innuendo and knew that wine and her affections would go a long way towards making him feel better. Her plans sounded good to him and he started to smile. As he looked at her, he took in her desirable figure. Even in her work boots, she was a fox. Her tight jeans and long hair had always been an attraction for him. The thinly veiled tease was a welcome enticement.

"Not so fast," interjected Alejandro. "We gotta figure this out."

"What do you mean?" Juan and DD said, almost in unison.

"Dude, you just got your ass kicked. We can't let this go. I'm calling some of the guys to meet us at The Beer Tap."

The Beer Tap was the local watering hole for men like them: rugged, hardworking, manly men. Men who loved beer and whiskey. For years, this had been Juan and Alex's favorite hangout after a hard day of work, cement and sweat.

"You're gonna go drink beer with the guys after what I just offered you?" She was genuinely hurt. Her charm usually worked on men, and, until now, it had worked flawlessly on Juan.

"Babe, we gotta figure this out," he said, sheepishly shrugging his shoulders. As he did, he winced in pain.

"Tonight!?" she questioned, with an intentional jab in her tone.

Alex intervened, "Yes, tonight. Juan just got blindsided by some thugs. Thugs with enough money to hire a suit. That means this is bigger than we all know. I need to make some calls and talk to a couple of guys."

She looked at Juan for a final decision. Juan knew it would piss her off, but he still nodded in agreement with Alex.

"Well fine! You boys go have your fun." She spun around and headed for her car. Sarcasm unfiltered came in her next statement, "I'll see you boys at work tomorrow." What she meant was:

> *You're both behaving like juveniles. Juan, don't come to my place after you get drunk. Go with your friends tonight, and, if I've gotten over it, maybe we'll talk at work tomorrow.*

It's amazing what a woman can say without saying it.

In the unfinished parking lot, it didn't take much for her to spin her wheels in one final protest. The flying dirt and pebbles peppered the two friends with tiny missiles. Reactively, they raised their arms, hoping to shield their faces.

When the dust cleared, Alex looked over at Juan, "You ready?"

"Dude, you know I'm always ready for a beer."

He was only a little hesitant with his next request.

"How 'bout I leave my work truck here? I can pick it up tomorrow. I'm hoping, since you got my ass kicked, you'll be willing to get me drunk and drive me home."

Alejandro grinned and said, "I'll be your designated driver... I mean DD tonight."

"Dude, that's a horrible joke. Let's go." They both appreciated the lighthearted banter as they climbed into Alex's truck.

On the drive to The Beer Tap, Juan Marc tried to describe the compassionate mystery man that stayed with him. He knew there was something about him. No matter how hard he tried, he just couldn't convey his thoughts to his friend. To Alex, Juan came across as confused and jumbled. But they were together as friends, and this fact alone made them both feel better.

CHAPTER 3

The Message

Masters stood pridefully, looking out the window of the 35th story, elegantly appointed office. He held his glass of Jack Daniels in his left hand, swirling the ice slowly. In his right, he held his Cuban cigar with an ease that reflected he had been handling them his whole life. He was reminiscing while he took in the view. He loved the lights of the city from his perch. He'd come to this office since he was a child. He fondly remembered playing on the floor with toy trucks as a small kid. Later, he remembered bringing his beautiful, blonde high school girlfriend to this office to impress her. A devilish grin emerged as he remembered that the entire evening with the young lady had worked out in his favor. He got what he wanted that night because he was as persuasive as his father. She was his first of many conquests, sexual and otherwise, in this office.

It was here that his dad met with many powerful and influential men. He had worked them masterfully with ruthless persuasion. Richard "Dick" Masters had always loved, yet feared, his father. His shrewdness had passed on nicely to Dick. Dick not only adopted the "lean heavy on the other guy" ways of his father, but he also lacked any sort of conscience that would constrain him with boundaries brought on by scruples. Fearless, icy and overbearing: he relished these traits. These characteristics had helped him parlay his Dad's company into a financial and political force. Sandie's Foundations was named after Dick's mom. She had helped his dad start the company. Sandie was the only one who could soften his hard-dealing father. When the door opened, it was an expected visitor.

"Lance."

"Sir."

"Did you get Mr. Fuente's attention?" asked Masters.

"I did as you asked," he replied with confidence.

"And the men?"

"I gave them each an extra thousand. Tomorrow, they'll be back on their job site with one of the crews, and I wanted to make sure that the events of the evening didn't come up in conversation. I also let them know that it would be a safety problem for them if it ever did come up. There are so many possibilities for accidents on the job sites," he said with a wicked smirk.

"So, you think they'll keep quiet?" Masters asked quickly, wanting to get on to the real matter at hand.

"I do."

"Good."

"I also took the liberty of acquiring a phone. I figured you'd want to make the call yourself." He knew his boss liked it when he anticipated his next step.

"Good. It's secure?"

"Of course," he nodded.

"Voice?"

"Sir, I would never hand you a phone without voice encryption. You know that," he said, dripping with hubris.

His pride diminished with Dick's next response.

"Lance, you know if you ever let me down, or expose me in any way, I'll personally see to it that you become a permanent part of one of our projects." Masters spoke without any disdain or threatening in his voice. The creepiest part was that it was so casual; as if it was as easy as pouring himself a glass of Tennessee whiskey. Lance was also quite confident that there were others who had let him down and had met similar fates.

"I know, sir." With that, Lance handed Masters the phone with the already pre-dialed number. In a moment, the connection was made.

At The Beer Tap, Alejandro sat at a back corner table. Above and behind the table was something like a basketball scoreboard. It was the only sports-related thing in the place. The rest of the bar was a typical dive bar: tables, booths, smoke, neon, pool tables and beer. Lots of beer.

The sign had a score: Visitors 3, Home 8. The guys at the table knew what the score meant, and they knew who they sat with. No one ever brought it up. It was unspoken among them because he wanted it that way. Eleven times, Alex had intervened: intervened in what he believed were moments of injustice. Either someone was being hassled, or an unfair fight had broken out. Regardless of the matter, Alejandro couldn't be a bystander if he believed something wasn't right. Each time this happened, he would find himself in the midst of a brawl. He was fierce and had a well-earned reputation for being both daring and capable. His reputation was such that, sometimes he could confront a situation by simply standing up. If the man or men were cowards, or if their resolve wavered, they would usually feign an excuse to back down. Eleven times, it had come to blows. Eight times, he had won. Three, he had lost. He never regretted any of them. After three or four fights, Sally, the owner, put the scoreboard on the wall. She did it because she liked it when Alex was in the bar.

Unofficially, this was his table and he was welcome anytime. His very presence meant a lot of nonsense never escalated.

Tonight, he was with three others. Juan, Lenny and Mark. They had all just heard Juan's story and he was already on his second beer.

Alex and Lenny were still on their first. Lenny, an old family friend, wasn't in the construction business. He did, however, have a knack for being at Alex's side when he needed him the most. Lifelong friends, there was an unspoken bond that meant dutifully looking out for one another.

Mark, on the other hand, was listening intently and peeling the label from his recently emptied bottle of Dasani. For some reason that none of them knew, Mark didn't drink. He always had a bottle of water. It seemed odd, but since he'd been around these guys for years, they didn't much care about his water addiction. He was the kind of guy that was always around construction sites. Sometimes, he had even worked for Alex, but he never stayed long. He was tatted on his arms and hands. Curiously, there was no ink on his neck or face. The group knew he'd fought in Iraq, but everyone respected him enough not to ask about it. He was valued by these men because he had a reputation as a tough worker. They all considered him a friend and welcomed him to the table.

When Alex's phone rang, no one was really surprised. They had all expected the call.

"Alex here," he answered crisply.

"Do I have your attention?" said the obviously encrypted and mutated voice.

"You had someone kick my friend's ass. Hell yeah, you got my attention."

"I thought it might."

"What's your name, asshole?"

"The better question is, what do I want?" Alex's attempt to get a name hadn't worked.

"What do you want? What's this all about?"

"There are some very powerful people that are working on the Madison Complex."

"Yes." Alex knew where this was going.

"They stand to make millions. Your two-bit concrete company stands in the way of their profits."

"You bastard, you beat up my friend and try to scare me away from a contract! My concrete company can't supply more than about a third of the concrete that's needed. You piece of shit. If this is about money, you and whoever hired you can kiss my ass."

"Mr. Marquez!" the voice said sharply.
It was enough to get Alex's attention.

"You understand that this was just the message. Your friend only suffered minor injuries. If you insist on competing with us, I can assure you the next mishap won't be as trivial."

Alex knew going further with this man meant angering someone very powerful. At this moment, though, he simply couldn't help it. He couldn't stand bullies. He was sick of a lifetime of people keeping him and his friends down. Something within him welled up from the deepest part of who he was.

"You son of a bitch. Are you threatening me!?" He didn't stop there, but he took a quick breath. "I'll kick your ass! Be a man and come see me yourself, you coward!" Another sharp breath. "Come on, let's go!"

"Mr. Marquez. Watch your back. Or rather, watch the backs of everyone you know."

At this last statement, Alex completely lost it, "You mothe..."

The line went dead.

His hands revealed his anger. He slammed his phone down and balled his fists. He looked each man in the eye one at a time. Around the table, they looked back with equal intensity. They had seen that look before and knew he wouldn't back down. They also knew to wait until he was ready to speak.

"Guys, this man just threatened us." He let this first statement sink in. "Not just us, but everyone we work with. I'm not gonna let anyone push us around."

His natural ability to lead was coming through. His intensity alone was inspiring, and these men wanted to go to battle with him. It was this same sentiment that had convinced each of these men, at different times, to help in previous skirmishes.

"Alex, man," Juan said quietly, "what's the play?"

Mark questioned, "Cops?" and looked at Alex for an answer.

"Lenny, cops?" asked Alex.

"Not a chance," was Lenny's reply.

"Did he say what this is all about?" asked Juan.

"Yeah, it's because we bid on the Madison Complex."

The Madison Complex was the biggest works project the city had ever invested in. The city council had purchased farmland on the north side of town. Hundreds of acres had been purchased from dozens of farmers and other folks that lived in that area. The grand design was to make it a destination location: hotels, restaurants, an indoor sports arena, outdoor football and baseball fields. There was even going to be a boardwalk on a man-made lake. The boardwalk would be complete with bright lights, shops, arcades and restaurants. At the furthest end, they would build an amusement park with a roller coaster, carousel and Ferris wheel. Construction of this magnitude would last two to three years and create thousands of blue-collar jobs. It would also make the owners of construction companies very wealthy. Everyone at the table knew that big, outside investors were behind it all.

"Alex?" Juan was the first to speak.

"Yeah, man?"

"Dude, you're one of a hundred sub-contractors that placed bids. Why are they coming after you? Why are they coming after us?"

"My guess," he was still processing it all himself, "is that there's either another concrete contractor out there that has some powerful friends, or the general contractor is trying to run it through a concrete company that he owns a piece of. Even if he's one of several owners, there's still millions upon millions of dollars to be made on concrete alone with a project this big." He sat back, still putting it all together. "At least that's my best guess."

"So, if we aren't going to the cops, and we're not gonna pull the bid, what do we do?"

"Mark, you've been working for other contractors lately. I figure you could continue working for them. Then you won't get caught up in any of this."

"Ah, hell no!"

"What do you mean?"

"Look, we all know my wife's sister is DD. No way she's gonna be in danger, and I sit this one out." Everyone could see he was committed.

It was true. Mark was married to Kathy, DD's sister. Now Alex understood. As a man of valor, Mark could never step aside.

"I honestly didn't see it like that. I was kinda hoping, for your sake, that you'd walk away. I don't want this to be any bigger than it has to be," Alex said, leaning back in his chair, continuing to think. "Well... since I can't convince you otherwise, I might as well offer you a job."

"That's more like it. Whatcha got for me?"

"Why don't you work with Juan? Can you drive a truck?"

"Yeah, man," replied Mark.

"Ok. Juan, you're the foreman. Mark, you drive one of our mixers." Both Mark and Juan nodded. Lenny sat quietly listening.

"Hey Mark, with your military background, I'd like to ask one more favor."

"What's that?"

"Keep your eyes and ears open for trouble." Alex looked at Mark intently.

"Are you cool if I pack?"

"It may, technically, be against company policy to have weapons in company vehicles, but I'm confident no one will be checking your truck."

Mark gave a single nod.

"So, Alex, what do we do tomorrow?" asked Juan Marc.

"We go to work as usual. We're behind, so we keep pouring concrete and catch up on our jobs. We have to keep our word to our clients."

With that, Lenny waved the waitress over. "Tab, please."

CHAPTER 4

Escalation

"I hope they know what they're doing," said DD, speaking into her phone.

Kathy responded, "When Mark came home last night and told me what was going on, I told him they needed to call the police."

"Yeah, I tried that this morning at the office with Alejandro and Juan. They totally blew me off."

"I just hope this was all a mistake and it blows over."

"I don't think so. Someone went to enough trouble to beat Juan and call Alex on an encrypted phone. I mean, who does that?"

"It could still be a mistake."

"It was all regarding Alex's bid for the Madison Complex concrete work. They knew way too much. There's no way it's a mistake."

Kathy couldn't argue her point any further. She knew her sister was right.

"DD?"

"Yeah, Sis."

"Why don't you consider staying at our place? I hate to think of you all alone with these threats being made. If these guys know Juan and Alex, they certainly know you. After all, you're joined at the hip with Alex at work and with Juan every night."

DD cherished her independence, especially the liberty to have Juan over at any time. The idea of staying with her sister and Mark was too much. She needed her privacy.

"Kathy, you're so kind. And I know you're just looking out for me. Juan is over here most nights, and I feel safe with him around. Besides, I keep Crockett with me at all times."

Crockett, Kathy knew, was DD's 9mm pistol. She'd had it for years. As a girl, she'd seen re-runs of Miami Vice. She always had a crush on Don Johnson. His character on the show was Sonny Crockett; hence, the name for her weapon was an affectionate one.

"At least think about it. You're welcome anytime," said Kathy, knowing she couldn't change her sister's mind, but remaining hopeful she would reconsider.

A discreet, two-tone *chirp* came over the phone. DD looked down. It was Juan Marc.

"Kathy, I gotta letcha go. Juan's on the other line."

"Ok girl. Love ya. Bye."

DD clicked over and started playfully teasing her lover. "Mr. Fuente, this is DD at the home office. What's your status?" she said in a sultry and frisky tone.

"Ms. McFearson, I'm back at the convenience store site. We were gearing up to pour our last slab, but the guys who were supposed to set the rebar didn't have it done," he replied, trying to focus on the problem at hand.

"I see. And just what would you like me to do about it?" she asked, coyly.

"How about you load the trailer up with rebar and ties and drive it over? Bring me some lunch. And bring me a cold drink with a hot kiss." He had started to play her game.

"I'll bring you something better than lunch and a kiss, but it has to wait until tonight!" She let that sink in. "Unless you want to hang out with your guy friends at The Beer Tap again?"

"Ouch, that hurt. Come on baby. You know I needed to be with them last night."

"I don't know any such thing. Remember, girls like me get tired of waiting. If you don't come around enough, I just might find another handsome young thing to replace ya." She said, half teasing and half serious.

"Baby, you wouldn't!" Juan jokingly protested.

"Boy, I was huntin' a man when I found you. Don't think for a minute that I can't hunt me another."

Beneath the innuendo and jousting, he knew that DD was a catch. He also knew that she could easily find someone else. She, after all, even in work clothes, was the hottest woman around. He had no intention of pushing her away.

"Ok, I surrender!" he said. She had made her point, and they both knew it. "Now, about the rebar?"

"I pulled up the inventory while you were squirming like a little kid. It looks like we don't have what you need in the yard," said DD. "Why don't you run over and pick some up at the hardware store? You can leave Mark there with the guys. The amount you need should fit in the back of your truck."

"Sounds good," he agreed.
They exchanged goodbyes and hung up. He really was looking forward to spending the evening with her. He loved her, but he hadn't found the right time to say it. To him, their relationship went way beyond the physical. He just couldn't keep his mind off her when they were apart. When they were together, he was enamored. He was smitten with her smile, her scent, her voice and even her happy-go-lucky and perky manner. Regardless of what you call it, DD was becoming his everything. He deeply hoped she felt the same way.

He walked over to brief Mark about his trip to the store. "I'll be back in an hour or so."

"Cool, man. See ya soon," replied Mark. He felt good being able to watch over the team. He also felt good about the .40 caliber Sig stashed in his truck.

Juan hopped in his JPR logoed work truck and drove away. He didn't know that he'd never see his crew or Mark again.

* * *

At the hardware store, Juan walked inside to the service desk. He knew the rebar and other construction materials were in the back.

"May I help you?" asked the man behind the counter. He noticed the wounds on his face and thought, *Dang! I wonder what happened to this guy?!*

"Yeah, I need thirty 3/8 by six-foot-long pieces of steel rebar," replied Juan.

The man typed quickly on his computer.

"Looks like we have what you need behind the building. Do you know how to get back there?"

"Yup. I'll pull my truck around."

"Sounds good. The usual guy back there is off today. I'm covering both, so I'll walk to the gate and let you in, and then I'll help you find it."

Juan nodded. "Got it. What do I owe ya?"

"With tax, three hundred ninety-two dollars and 23 cents."

"That's fine. Put this on the Just Plain Rocks corporate account."

When they finished their transaction, Juan headed out to his truck and pulled around to the gate.

The man had already made it from the service counter and was holding the gate open at the side of the building. As Juan passed by, he rolled his window down.

"It's in the far back, right corner. I'll be there in a minute. There's a truck behind you. I need to see if he has an order back here, too."

Juan drove through, and the next truck drove up. It was an especially large ¾ ton truck with six guys in the large crew cab. They all looked grubby and fresh from the job site. The driver handed a receipt over for various sizes of lumber.

"You guys been here before?"

"Yeah, we know where everything is. We can find it."

"Ok, I'm gonna help this other guy. Let me know when you're done. I need to match the lumber count with your receipt."

"That's fine," said the driver dismissively.

The driver was a steely-eyed, forty-something. He'd been around the block and was salty from his years of hard labor. He was tired of construction, and some days he wanted to be anywhere but the job site. His body was strong, but he didn't have the endurance he did when he was twenty years younger. The guys he was with all relished the trip off the job site. It meant a few hours out of the sun. They all also wanted the extra cash for this special project. Besides, all he had to do was, "break a bone, or cut him a little." His orders were clear. Hurt the man, but don't kill him. He looked in his rearview mirror to see if anyone else was coming in.

All clear, he thought.

He didn't know that the man who had arranged this special project was in the main parking lot. He was there, waiting and watching.

In the car sat the man who Juan had come to know as the angry accountant. He watched as the truck went through the gate. He thought for a moment that the driver had looked back at him with his rearview mirror. No matter. It was time to update Masters. He picked up his phone and hit the speed dial.

"They're in. Juan's here just like my source said," and the conversation continued.

Back in the warehouse yard, Juan made his way to the area he'd been given directions to. As he drove up, he saw a familiar frame. A large man stood there looking down at the different sizes of rebar. Juan recognized him as the man that had watched over him the day before. Juan wanted to thank him and introduce himself. He almost stumbled as he jumped out of the truck.

"Hey, mister!" Juan called.

The man turned and looked at him with deep hollowed eyes which caused him to pause. The next call to the man was more subdued and restrained. Somehow, Juan knew this man was averse to loud and boisterous talk.

"Mister, do you remember me?" Juan said, putting his hand out. "I wanted to thank you for what you did yesterday."

The man looked intently at Juan's face. "It looks like it still hurts."

"It does, man. Last night, I drank a six-pack and took half a bottle of ibuprofen just so I could sleep." Although his new friend's expression never wavered from his kind smile, Juan became self-conscious. He felt like he was in the presence of someone very benevolent and strong. Although he couldn't put his finger on it, he wanted what this man had. The mystery deepened. Who was this guy?

"Forgive me for not introducing myself. My name is Juan Marc," he said, trying to continue the conversation.

"Eli! What are you doing here?" asked the man from the service desk as he approached. He was grinning and the two seemed to be old friends. Juan didn't know what was going on.

The man returned the welcome with a huge smile as he stuck out his hand, "Mac! Great to see you, my friend."

"You two know each other?" asked Juan.

"We met a few months ago. Eli just seems to show up at the right place at the right time," said the man addressed as Mac.

"Uh...yeah... I know what you mean. He helped me out just yesterday." Again, Juan stuck out his hand towards the man. "Eli, it's good to know your name."

"So, what brings you here?" asked Mac.

"This guy," motioning towards Juan.
Both men were perplexed. Juan spoke first.

"What do you mean?"

"I'm here for you, my friend. I'm here because I want to help."

"Help me buy rebar?"

"No. It's more than that."

The truck had made two or three passes by them while this conversation was taking place. The steely-eyed man was making sure no other customers were around, and the cameras weren't pointed where he and his guys would be. Once he felt confident, he pulled up near Juan, Mac and Eli.

"Mac, I'm here for you as well." His look was calm and compassionate.

Neither Juan nor Mac understood what Eli was talking about. They both started to question him, but he looked up at the truck that had just stopped. They followed his gaze. It only took a moment for all six men to exit the truck. The men held various weapons that you'd find on a construction site. Some had tools, like hammers and wrenches and Steel Eyes had clenched fists. There was no mistaking their intent. Juan, having just taken a beating the day before, was immediately on the defense. He looked at Mac and Eli. Both men were calm but guarded.

Mac, feeling like he represented the store, spoke first. "May I help you gentleman?"

One of the men spoke, "We got no beef with you or him," he said, pointing at Eli. "We just need to have a little talk with Juan."

Juan was shaken at this turn of events. He knew this wouldn't turn out well.

"Not again," said Juan. The other, more tactical part of his brain thought, *At least I see this one coming.*

Eli stepped forward calmly. He was intentional about appearing non-threatening.

"Guys, Juan's with me. If you want to talk, then talk," Eli hoped they would reconsider and back down.

"Get out of our way, and you won't get hurt," came a sharp reply.

"Hey guys, let's not do this. He's just here picking up some supplies," said Mac.

Juan Marc was looking around for something, anything that might give him an advantage. He reached over and grabbed a three-foot-long piece of rebar, and he noticed his palms were already beginning to sweat. The bar was heavy and solid, so he tightened his grip. This time he wouldn't go down without a fight.

Eli motioned for Juan to stay back and said, "Men, you say you want to talk with Juan. State your business and move on."

A voice from the pack of guys said, "An ass whippin' is our message."

A couple of the guys snickered as they began to move to surround the three. Steel Eyes noticed Juan had picked up the rebar. He knew he would use it to fight back and the other two weren't showing signs of backing down. He was thinking this needed to start before the other two picked up weapons as well. Things weren't going to be as easy as he had hoped. Still, he wanted to get paid.

"I'm gonna give you one last chance to walk away. Otherwise, you'll get the same message he does," he said, motioning towards Juan.

"Eli, you good?" said Mac. Eli knew what Mac was asking.

"I'm good. You?"

They both nodded, knowing what was about to happen.

It was one of the young guys who started it all. He charged Mac with a pipe wrench. Mac's instincts kicked in. He stepped sideways to avoid the wrench and, as the kid passed by, punched him in the nose so hard that his feet flew up in the air. His upper body and head smacked the pavement with bone jarring malice. He was out cold.

In a blink, the others rushed Juan and Eli. Eli was a bear of a man. He used his fists and went toe to toe with the men that were trying to gang up on him.

A couple of the older guys were still trying to fulfill the mission of getting to Juan. Juan was swinging the rebar like a bat and he had the ferocity of a wounded animal.

As the brawl continued, it was the attackers that had the upper hand. They leveraged their numbers by striking from the sides and behind. There were too many to watch and defend against. They circled like wolves waiting for each man to face off, then someone would come in from behind and deliver blows to their legs and backs.

One of the young guys got too close to Eli and paid dearly with a powerful right hook to the chin. The man's head twisted in a violent snap and crumbled at Eli's feet.

Juan, Eli and Mac were trying to watch and defend without over committing. They knew standing toe to toe with any one man would only leave their backs vulnerable.

Eli looked over at Mac just as a pipe came crashing down on his skull. Mac was stunned for a moment, and he began to stagger. Then something clicked in Mac; anger and hatred that he hadn't felt since the war rose up in him. As a former Marine, he'd seen combat in the Middle East. He was formidable before, but now he was devastatingly ferocious. Like flipping a light switch, he became the hunter instead of the prey. His attack was a blur of punches and kicks. He grabbed the pipe from the man who'd hit him. He dropped down to a kneeling position and, with all his might, smashed the man's knee.

Three down. Now it was man to man.

Juan had been hit several times, but he'd given some, too. He was facing the steely-eyed man, holding his rebar like a sword as he held the man at bay. The man was cautious but kept pressing closer, hoping Juan would make a mistake. A series of fake lunges by his attacker caused Juan to swing and miss several times. Again, the man darted in aggressively as if to attack. Convinced the attack was real, Juan swung with all his might. As before, the man dodged back to evade the blow, causing Juan to over-extend himself with the heavy bar. For a moment, he was off balance and torqued sideways. The man saw the opening he'd been waiting for and pounced on his victim. Both men crashed hard on the concrete. Battered, they punched, kicked and tried to get position on the other.

Eli caught his assailant's arm and wrenched it with force. The man screamed in pain and the hammer he had been using fell with a *clank.* Now it was a boxing match. Eli's punches were faster and harder than the man expected. The young construction worker tried to throw counter punches of his own, but it was becoming clear Eli was gaining momentum.

Mac had been trading jabs and his arms were starting to burn with fatigue. His accoster was massive, and he was proving resilient to Mac's repeated blows to his body and face. He adjusted his target and landed a fist to his throat. The man crumpled, gasping for air and clutching his gullet.

Juan and Steel Eyes were feverishly wrestling on the ground, each man working to gain an advantage.

From the corner of his eye, a knife flashed, and Juan felt it penetrate between his ribs. His initial reaction was to grab the man and pull him closer, hoping he couldn't continue to swing the blade. He pulled him in tight. They faced each other with savage intensity, both knowing that death hung in the balance. The man's arms were now equally wrapped around Juan. He repositioned the knife in his hand and began to plunge it into his back. Juan felt the searing pain and began to gasp as he struggled to get air. He started coughing blood. He knew he was in trouble, but he just couldn't breathe.

Mac surveyed the group.

Four down. Eli looks like he's getting the better of his guy. And then he saw Juan. The man was plunging a knife over and over into his back. It looked like a vicious hug of blood and violence. Mac grabbed the rebar that Juan had dropped, and he came down hard on the man's head. The man never saw it coming and hadn't even tried to brace himself for the blow. With one swipe, Mac had neutralized him. He collapsed limp next to Juan, and the flurry of stabs ceased.

Mac looked up to see Eli give a final knockout blow. Down went the man who lay bleeding.

Mac turned aside and knelt to help Juan. He tried to hold his head up, but Juan was choking on his own blood.

He instinctively rolled him onto his side so he could spit it out.

"Are you OK?!" Mac asked, already knowing the answer.

"I'll call 911," said Eli, pulling his phone out.

"I can't..." Juan gasped. "I can't breathe."

Mac knew from the location of the stab wounds that Juan likely had a collapsed lung. He was probably getting blood into the chest cavity as well. Without medical help, he would die.

"Eli, where's the ambulance?"

"On their way."

Eli knelt next to Juan. "Dear God, help this man."

Even then, Eli and Mac could tell the life was draining out of him. Juan desperately looked to Mac, who was still holding him.

Then he locked on to Eli's gaze. "Who are you?" he said, his voice raspy from the blood.

"I'm here for you," is all Eli responded. His very presence was reassuring. Juan felt Eli place his large warm hand on his cheek compassionately. Its gentle strength cut through the chaos, fear and pain. And, in that moment, he felt complete peace as his life evaporated away.

The man in the car in the parking lot heard the sirens and saw the ambulances and police pulling into the parking lot. He started his car, drove to the nearest exit and pulled out into traffic.

CHAPTER 5

The Fallout

Mac was tired of waiting. He had been sitting on this gurney for hours. First the nurses, then the doctor and finally, the police had wanted to see him. He did have bumps, bruises, aches and pains, but mostly, he was angry at the whole situation. He had started his day simply being an ordinary employee at a hardware store. Now, even though he had prevailed, he felt like a victim. Someone had come into his domain and gotten the better of him. More than that, he felt responsible for the dead man. The man was in his area of responsibility. He had similar lingering feelings from the war. If ever someone was hurt or killed while he was on duty, he always felt an overwhelming sense of obligation. He couldn't shake the feeling that he had somehow let them down, and today's emotions were same.

He wondered what Eli was going through. He had only met Eli a few times, but they had become quick friends as Eli's gentle nature made it easy to do so. He was hoping Eli hadn't felt interrogated the way he had. Luckily, there was a local roofer who had just come in behind the warehouse to pick up supplies and had seen the whole thing. When things started to escalate, he pulled out his phone and recorded the incident. After much discussion and review of the video, the authorities concluded that Mac and Eli were not the instigators. Still, right now, Mac wanted to go home and pour himself a glass of Jim Beam.

* * *

At Just Plain Rocks, word had spread quickly. It was DD who had taken the initial call. She held her composure enough to walk into Alex's office and give him the news. As she finished, her heart physically ached as she crumbled into the nearest chair and began to weep.

Alex, on the other hand, stood and angrily paced the room. He wanted to know what happened, how it happened and who had done this to his beloved friend. He needed details.

DD was lamenting her friend and lover. Normally strong and resilient, she felt weak, scared and overwhelmed by her loss.

Alex started to reach for the phone to call the police for more information. Just as his hand reached the receiver, it rang. It startled him, but in his anger and adrenaline rush, he put the phone to his ear and barked, "What!?"

"Mr. Marquez. I hope you now see how serious I was about our conversation yesterday."

"You bastard!"

"You seem to think that calling me names will stop me. Something so trivial has never stopped me," he said, dripping condescension.

"I'm gonna find out who you are and kill you myself!"

"You'll do no such thing. The bids close for these projects next Tuesday, the 12th. The decision will be made on who gets the contracts after that. It's my expectation that you will withdraw your bid by Tuesday at five p.m. If you choose to bid against us, you know what we're capable of."

It had pained Alex to listen to this. He wanted to shut this guy up. Alejandro, however, was sharp-witted, and he was hoping to keep the man talking so he might give away some detail, some bit of information that might help him figure out who this guy was. He hated to continue the conversation, but he tried to ask questions anyway.

"Can we come to some sort of agreement?" asked Alex, in a much more level tone. "Tell me what you really want."

"Nice Try."

At this final statement, the line went dead.

Alex turned to DD who had tried to piece together what was being said. After a brief review of the call, Alex had gotten her up to speed. DD's sadness had become mixed with anger.

* * *

Alex, who had known Juan's family for many years, felt obligated to break the news to them. He drove to their home, a home where Juan and Alex spent much of their childhood together: sleepovers, movies, games and meals. They'd been friends, it seemed like to Alex, since the beginning of time. The hardest conversation he ever had was telling Juan's mom and dad that he had been murdered. Tears flowed and vain attempts were made to console each other. After a while, Alex left Juan's parents to grieve in their own way. He was emotionally exhausted as he drove back to JPR to check on DD.

When he arrived, he found that DD had done what DD does best. She tracked down the hospital that had received Juan's body. She and Alejandro both grabbed their keys, quietly locked up the office, got into their separate cars and went to say their final goodbyes.

CHAPTER 6

The Three Unite

Three days later, under a gray sky, friends, family and coworkers all stood around as the Catholic priest performed a traditional ceremony for Juan. The minister kept his comments relatively generic as he had never really known Juan. Yes, Juan had been to Mass a few times, but he had never been a regular attendee. The priest encouraged everyone to take time to mourn and pray for their lost loved one. There were heart wrenching sobs and tears throughout the group. No one, however, lamented more vocally than Juan's mother. You could see on her face the anguish and loss. Her sobs pierced, to the core, everyone in attendance. Alex watched his friend's mother in her agony, and he again had this thing well up inside him. It was an intense sense of vengeance. He needed justice for Juan's folks.

This desire for vengeance was being seared deep into Alex's soul. As the ceremony ended and people respectfully walked back to their vehicles, he was trying to figure out how to find this man. He was deep in thought when a large, but gentle, hand touched his right shoulder. He turned around, somewhat dazed, and saw a mountain of a man he had never met before. The man stuck out his great paw and Alex, in return, took it. They shook hands briefly as both men looked down, humbly and reverently, at the ground.

"My name is Eli. I was one of the men with your employee when this happened. I'm so sorry for your loss," said Mr. Seahur.

In the days leading up to the funeral, Alex had visited the local police department. He had been allowed to watch the video the roofer had provided to the investigators. He recognized this man standing in front of him. This man had fought to protect Juan. To Eli's left was another man. He, too, stuck out his hand.

"I'm sorry for your loss as well."

"I recognize you two from the video the cops showed me. I guess I owe you my gratitude. I'm grateful for you both. Juan was more than just an employee; he's been my friend since we were kids." He was trying to hold back his tears as he spoke.

He looked intently at their faces and noticed these two men, although together, had very different demeanors. Eli seemed sad and humble. Mac, on the other hand, seemed frustrated and angry. It was Mac who spoke next.

"Mr. Marquez, I know your friend died. For that I'm sorry, but we got our tails kicked, too. I want to find out what this is all about. I don't mean to interrupt your time of mourning, but if you have any idea what's going on, I'd appreciate it if you'd fill me in."
As he said this, it came out in a very mixed tone. He was trying to be respectful, and at the same time, he was angry. The need for more information burned in him like a consuming fire.

"I didn't catch your name, mister," said Alex to Mac.

"Mac Stephens. Pleased to know you," as he stuck out his hand again.

"You tried to help my friend; for me, that's a big deal. I'd like to buy you both lunch tomorrow. It'll be a much more appropriate time to have this conversation and I'll tell you everything I know then."

"Mr. Marquez, thank you for the offer. What I know today is enough. I have no desire to pursue it further, so I'm going to respectfully decline your invitation," said Eli.

"Suit yourself."

"I'll meet with you. Name the time and place, and I'll be there," said Mac.

Over the next couple of minutes, they made lunch arrangements and committed to seeing each other the next day. Without a word, they walked to their cars and headed home for the evening.

* * *

The next day, it was sunny and hot, and Alex had chosen a restaurant which had an outside patio. Conversely, Mac wished they had selected an inside table, but Alex had a purpose for being outside. No one else dared to sit out in the +100° heat, and Alex wanted to be able to speak freely. He had seen this man fight in the video and wanted him on his side. Alex needed allies, and Mac just might be motivated and skilled enough to be of value.

The two had settled in and ordered a couple of beers. Mac was taken slightly aback when Alex told the waitress that one more would be joining their party. They would wait to order till then. Mac couldn't have anticipated what he saw next.

Entering the patio was a woman so attractive that, when he looked at her, he couldn't help but gasp. She was stunning. She was wearing a nice fitting silk shirt to avoid the heat. Her denim jeans fit well in all the right places and cowboy boots completed the look. Mac couldn't take his eyes off her, and he was coming to grips with the realization that she was heading for their table. As she neared, she spoke.

"Hey, Alex, it's crazy hot. Why did you want to eat on the patio?"

"Because nobody else is insane enough to be out here," he said, standing up.

He gave her a quick, platonic, welcoming hug as if she were a sister. Mac still couldn't talk, but he stood up and put his hand out.

"You must be Mac?"

"That's me. And you are?" he said, dying to know her name, but trying to play it cool.

"I'm DD. Alex showed me the video. I came today to thank you for helping Juan."

"You knew him?" asked Mac.

"Well... Yes, as a matter of fact. We started out as coworkers." She looked down at the table and fiddled with her napkin.

Mac could tell there was more to this. He knew she was hurting, but he wanted to know more. There was a pause in the conversation while the waitress approached and took their orders. Mac could see the tears beginning to well up in her eyes as she continued.

"Over this last several months, we had been dating. It was better than I could've imagined. We started to have conversations about moving in together and maybe getting engaged." She started to sob, her face displayed her anguish, and she struggled through one last thought before she burst into tears. "It's all gone now. It's over, and none of those dreams will ever come true."

Alex interceded. "Take your time, DD."

"Yeah.... Take your time," uttered Mac, who had come to realize that this woman was in real pain. She was a wounded soul and he knew she needed time to heal. From that moment on, he thought of her as Juan's girlfriend.

They all sat quietly, and, in a few moments, the food came. They were halfway through their meal when Alex looked up at Mac. It wasn't an ordinary look, rather a "look him over" sort of thing. He was sizing him up. On the video, this man had handled himself quite well. As crude as it was, Alex wondered if he could whip him in a bar fight. The consummate fighter, Alex, of course, concluded that he would win. Nevertheless, it would still be good to have a man like this working with them. It was time to get to the point.

"Mac, I want you to know this wasn't some random act of violence."

"I figured there was more to it. People don't randomly come to hardware stores to start fights. I gotta know why all of this happened."

"The day before you and Eli were drawn into this, Juan was jumped on one of our worksites. He took a beating that would have sent most people to the hospital."

"That explains his messed-up face."

Over the next ten minutes, Alejandro described the events of the day before: the assault at the work site and the phone call he had received. He also told Mac about the call the day of Juan's murder. As he related the story, Mac listened carefully. Mac's own sense of justice was being stirred. He shifted from sharing empathy with DD to sharing anger with Alejandro. By the time the story was finished, Mac was shifting in his seat, and his brow was furled in anger.

"I'm gonna need another drink," declared Mac. "This time something harder. Waitress... I'll take a shot of Jim Beam."

As the waitress went to get his drink, he nodded for Alex to continue.

"Mac, why did you come here today?"

"I needed to know why I got my ass kicked. Now that I know, I'm more pissed than ever."

"I'm pissed, too," agreed Alex.

They both paused while the waitress brought his drink. He downed the shot and looked Alex in the eye.

"So, what are we going to do about it?"

Alex replied, "I'm glad you asked. I was hoping you'd help us."

At this, DD sat up straighter. "I'm angry too, but what can we do?"

"We take the fight to this bastard!" said Alex. "We keep our bid in place because, when this is over, I want him to know he lost. Besides, leaving the bid active may draw him out."

At this point in the conversation, they started to get deeper into the details. They started working on a plan to figure out who this creep was. After the plan was formed, there was one final conversation.

"If we commit to this, we all understand the risks. One person has already died, which means he's not afraid to kill. If we do this, we risk each of our lives and others' as well," said Mac.

DD and Alex looked at one another. They knew Mac was right. Somewhere in their anger, sadness and sense of justice, they knew the task was inescapable. DD spoke for both of them.

"Mac, you're right about the risks. But I won't be able to sleep at night if this guy gets away with murder. Let's kick his ass!"

Alex didn't say a word. He simply raised his beer toward the center of the table. The other two raised their drinks as well. From this point on, they were all in.

CHAPTER 7

Masters Doubles Down

Stacy was busily typing on her computer when she sensed a presence. She glanced up from her desk and noticed the large man standing in front of her. She wondered how he got in because she hadn't heard the door. Her immediate impression was that he was a kind soul. When he began to speak, he was very plain, calm and, even though he was unrefined, the word that came to her mind was "gracious".

"May I help you?"

"Ma'am, may I speak to Mr. Masters, please?" said Eli.

"He doesn't see anyone without an appointment."

"I understand," he said with a calming smile. He paused for a moment before he continued. "Miss, may ask your name?"

"I'm Stacy."

"Stacy, it's my pleasure to meet you," as he extended his hand. "I'm Eli... Eli Seahur."

As they shook hands, Stacy realized there was something different about this man. He had an incredible, soothing effect. She felt peaceful and reassured. He had an air about him. In that moment, she became disarmed and dropped all her normal, protective mechanisms.

"Stacy, Mr. Masters and I go way back. I'm sure he won't mind that I dropped in."

For anyone else, she would have been unwilling to approach her overly demanding boss. Masters had given her explicit instructions on how to handle such things. For this new friend, though, she would make an exception. She reached for the phone and punched a couple of buttons.

"Mr. Masters, I'm sorry to bother you, but there is a gentleman here to see you."

"Lance is 10 minutes early?"

"No, sir. A Mr. Eli Seahur is here."

"Show him in."

Stacy thought, *This guy must be important*, as she hung up the phone.

She looked up at Eli and said with a smile, "Mr. Masters will see you now." She stood and opened the door to Masters' office.

"Thank you, Stacy. I appreciate your help."

"Eli, good to see you, old friend!" said Masters. "What brings you here today?"

They exchanged a brief handshake. Masters was smiling, trying to set a positive tone. He had dealt with Eli before. They met as children in this very office. Eli was the son of the cleaning woman that used to work in this building. As a child, Eli would help his mom by carrying trash, vacuuming and dusting. Over time, they developed a friendship. Sometimes, when Dick's father was away on business, all pride and pretense would be dropped, and only then were they allowed to play together. As adults, they had gone their separate ways. They both missed one another, but both men knew their paths were headed in opposite directions.

"Richard," said Eli, "you know who I work for, right?"

Masters had hoped Eli was here socially. He always hated these rabbit trails Eli tried to take him down. Eli would speak in what Dick would call "riddles." He never could quite understand what Eli was trying to say. It was always a waste of time that he considered a great annoyance.

"I know who you think you work for. You think you work for God," he said, as he stared at Eli.

"True."

"Eli, to be honest, I think you're a little off. It's kind of arrogant to think that you work for God. You and I grew up together. We played together and that's the only reason you're sitting in my office."

"You don't have to believe it, and thank you for seeing me today. But I'm here with a specific message." Eli wanted Dick's full attention.

"Now, what kind of message could your boss possibly want to give me?"

Without a moment of hesitation, Eli spoke. His voice was large and booming. His very countenance changed. He commanded the room completely, and it was as if even the inanimate objects were provoked to attention.

"You have spilled blood. I have seen and known your deeds. The stench of your wickedness I will only tolerate for a short time more. Once this time is complete, I will avenge this blood."

"Have you lost your mind!? Who do you think you are coming in here saying these things to me? Do you know what I can do to you? Take your crazy riddles and get the hell out of my office."

"Would you like me to take out your trash?"

"What the hell are you talking about?" Masters was puzzled by Eli's question. He was still seething from what he said.

"I noticed the waste bin by your desk is full, and I'm happy to take it on my way out."

Dick's head was spinning. He couldn't understand why this man would want to take out his trash. It seemed like lunacy. The problem was that Eli seemed so genuine in his offer. There appeared to be no motive or agenda.

"Eli, you should know better than anyone that I have people clean this office every night. Take your crazy 'message' and get out!" As he said this, Masters walked to the door and opened it. He motioned for Eli to leave.

"Dick, thank you for your time."

As Eli passed Stacy, he noticed another man waiting in the lobby; a guy in a suit who looked professional except for the grim aura about him. He waved his hand gently towards Stacy, thanked her and said goodbye.

Lance watched the man exit.

Masters, already standing at his office door, said, "Lance, get in here."

Lance and Dick entered the office and closed the door. Stacy sat there wondering what had just happened.

"What was that all about?" asked Lance.

"That guy's mom used to be a janitor here. We played together when we were kids. He's kind of an oddball now, but he stops by occasionally. He speaks in riddles like a freak, but he's harmless really."

"Oh...okay. Are you ready for an update?"

"Yeah, go ahead," he said, settling in behind his desk.

"Our sources tell us that none of the six guys have told the authorities anything. Likely, it's because I set the whole thing up through text messages on a burner phone. They don't even know who hired them. So far, we're in the clear."

"Good job. Any word on whether or not JPR pulled their bid?"

"Our inside guy told me that the bid has not been retracted." He looked at Dick to see how he would react.

"Well, they have the remainder of this week and the weekend, but hopefully they'll have pulled it by next Tuesday."

"Dick, why is this one bid so important to you?" Masters pivoted in his chair, turned his back to Lance and looked out the window. He looked as if he were trying to find the right words. Or maybe he was deciding whether to tell Lance the story at all. After an awkward pause, Masters spoke.

"Lance, if you ever tell anyone what I'm about to tell you, I'll kill you."

"I understand."

Masters turned around to face Lance and began to speak.

The reason my father did so well was because he was associated with a powerful family on the East Coast. His association with them was one of convenience, rather than financial. It was because people knew he had the support of this family that he was able to get things done that he couldn't have otherwise. Some people were intimidated by the very fact that he was involved with them. It made many, otherwise strong men, cowards, and it made my father wealthy. This same family approached me 18 months ago. They told me they had been backing my father for years. Now, they are looking for the payoff. In their estimation, the least I can do is ensure that they get the big construction contracts on the Madison Complex. The favorite son of the head of the family happens to own a concrete company. It was made clear to me that his son would be the one receiving the final contract for all the concrete work. I intend to make sure nothing stands in the way of him getting what he's asked for. If I don't, they'll think that, after years of protecting my father, they didn't get a return on their investment. They didn't have to threaten me. We all understand that if I don't deliver, I'll wake up at the bottom of the river with concrete shoes.

"Dick, am I to assume that since you and I are associated, I'm at risk as well?"

"Yes. That's the only reason I told you. Well, that and the fact that I want you to re-double your efforts."

"Since that's the case, might I make a suggestion?"

"And what would that be?"

"There's a woman that works with Alejandro Marquez. From what my sources tell me, she is the one that knows everything about his business. She's also beautiful. Looking at the world from his perspective, I can't think of any other relationship that may have more leverage with him. We could play it several ways." After this last statement, he looked at Masters as if asking for permission.

"What do you have in mind?"

"Kidnapping is too messy, and we really don't have a good place to keep her. An assault like with Juan would just raise more red flags with the authorities. I suggest a well-informed and detailed threat. A call or an email from an untraceable account would be a start. We can let her know that we know where she lives and remind her that Juan was just the beginning."

"I like the idea because it doesn't require any action beyond the threat. The risk is low if we're careful about how the message is delivered. Her move will be to tell Alex and he'll be forced to decide how much risk he's ready for her to endure."

"Yes, that's the idea. We need to make sure he's worried about those who are close to him. He knows from experience that we're capable of following through. So... may I have your approval to proceed?"

"Yes, proceed. Do it by email to change things up. Make sure it's untraceable. Scare her so bad that she'll be pleading with Alex to pull the bid."

Dick was even more sinister than Lance knew. He unknowingly grinned when he pictured in his mind the woman on her knees in front of Alex, begging him to pull the bid. He enjoyed the dominance of the scene. He secretly wished the woman would be in front of him begging for her life.

"Okay Dick, I have my orders. May I go now?"

"Just one last thing. Send the message today. If, by Monday afternoon, they haven't pulled the bid, make sure she's dead by Tuesday morning. I don't care how you do it, as long as it's clean."

"Understood," Lance said, exiting the room.

CHAPTER 8

Threat Received

DD hadn't slept well. She rolled over and turned off her alarm. It was six-thirty a.m., and she could already smell the coffee coming from her kitchen. She had set it to start each morning at six-fifteen because she loved the smell when she woke up. Her sleep had been restless and fraught with unnerving dreams. She got out of bed and fought through the fatigue just to get downstairs to the kitchen. She grabbed the cup she had set out the night before and began to pour. She loved the look of the steam drifting up as she filled her mug.

She leaned against the counter and, without even thinking, pulled her phone from her robe pocket. She often started her day by scrolling through work emails. She noted an email from the hardware store where a purchase had been made, but the product was never acquired. It didn't take her long to realize that it was the rebar Juan never picked up. This made her mind reel. Her stomach felt heavy and sick thinking about Juan again.

On the practical side though, she still needed to make sure the rebar got to the job site.

I'll talk to Alex about that later, she told herself.

She continued to scroll through as usual but noticed an unfamiliar email address in her inbox. She clicked it open and began to read. Before she got to the end, she was already gripped by fear. She steadied herself on the counter as her mind tried to process what she had read. She became self-conscious and looked around the room. She walked over to the drapes and closed them quickly. As scared as she was, she gathered her courage and peeked through the curtain just to be sure no one was out there.

Nothing unusual, she thought.

Her legs trembled as she made her way upstairs to her bedroom. She knelt next to the side of her bed and pulled out a lockbox. It didn't take long before she had Crockett in hand. She inserted the magazine and chambered the first round. She retreated to the corner and sat on the floor, gun pointed shakily at the door, even though there was no threat.

She sat motionless for what seemed like an eternity. At the same time, it felt like no time at all had passed. Eventually, she realized she couldn't sit there forever. She pulled her phone back out. With one hand pointing her gun, she used the other to speed dial Alejandro Marquez.

It didn't take long to fill Alex in on the email. Alex's sense of justice and protectiveness welled up in him as it had many times before.

Alex's last statement was, "I'm on my way!"

* * *

Alex was driving his JPR truck as quickly as he could. As he drove, he commanded the onboard system to call Mac Stephens. Within moments, Alex had given him the details. Now, Mac was on his way as well. They agreed to meet a block from DD's to game plan in case someone was watching the house.

Mac was already standing next to his truck when Alex arrived.

"Hey, Alex."

"Hey Mac, how long have you been here?"

"Not more than a minute or two." Both men's eyes were looking down the street.

"See anything?"

"No, not yet," Mac replied.

"Let's go get her."

"Not so fast."

"Why not? We need to get to DD."

"Always recon first," he said with a steady confidence. "We can't see much from here, so we'll have to do a drive-by and take a look. You take the street, and I'll take the alley." Alex nodded, and Mac jumped in his truck. "Alex, give DD a call and let her know that we're here. Hopefully, that'll make her feel better. Tell her, if all is clear, we'll be knocking on the front door in about five minutes. We'll regroup on the next block. If you see something, we can decide how we're going to deal with it together. Don't do anything on this first pass."

"I'm calling DD now. I'll see you in a few minutes," responded Alex, as they both drove off.

Alex started off down the street. His senses were heightened as he looked for any sign or person that might be out of the ordinary. As he drove through this typical, middle American neighborhood, he looked in every car and in between every house that he could. He half expected to see some man sitting in a black sedan wearing sunglasses across the street from DD's house like in the movies. In the end, he saw nothing of note.

Mac's experience was similar, although several of the backyards had barking dogs. It was early morning on a weekday; he assumed that everyone was either getting ready for work or had already left. The neighborhood was quiet.

They rendezvoused on the next block. They were both curious about what each other had seen.

"I didn't see anything from the alley," said Mac, starting the conversation.

"I got nothin'."

"Did you call DD?"

"Yeah, man, I did. She's okay but anxious for us to get there," said Alex.

"Okay, we play it cool. Let's just both pull up in front of her place and act like it's a normal visit."

Two minutes later, they had parked in the street and were taking the walkway up to her house.

"Stop!" Mac said as he grabbed Alex by the arm.

"What is it?!"

"I didn't see it from the street but there's a brown paper bag next to her door."

Alex stood still, wondering what to do.

"Let's move back to the street," Mac said, motioning for a retreat.

Back behind their vehicles, they knelt down.

"Call her and ask if she knows about the bag," Mac said to Alex.

Alex pulled out his phone and hit the speed dial.

"DD, we're out front in the street. When we walked up, we noticed a brown sack next to the door. Do you know what it is?"

"Oh, I'm so sorry. One of my neighbors told me that they were going to leave some apples for me."

"You think it's apples?"

"Well, I'm not completely sure, but that's my guess."

"Look DD, can you call your neighbor and make sure? Neither of us wants to take a chance."

"I'll call him then call you back.

Less than a minute later, Alex's phone began to ring. He swiped to answer.

"What'd you find out?"

"All I got was a voice mail. Alex, I'm sure it's just apples."

"Hang on a sec," said Alex.

"Mac, DD's convinced it's just apples."

"Maybe I'm just edgy. This is the kind of stuff we'd look for overseas. A plain sack on the side of the road was always considered a booby trap. I still don't like it."

"Dude, this is America. How many IED's have you heard of here."

"I still don't like it. Why don't we have her come out the back door?

"Because, it's apples and I believe her. We can't let these guys ruin our lives."

"It's an unnecessary risk."

"You know what. I'll go."

Alex put his phone to his ear, "DD, I'm gonna check it out. I'll call you back in a minute."

"We can still use the back door," said Mac.

"It's just apples," said Alex, turning to move up the sidewalk.

Mac couldn't believe his arrogance, but all he could do was watch. Alex slowed when he reached the steps up to the porch. Mac's heart was racing as he watched his new friend reach down and gingerly open the top of the sack and peek in. He knew it would explode. Alex plunged his hand in an pulled out a fat, bright red apple. He held it up for Mac to see. Mac exhaled hard. He hadn't even realized that he had stopped breathing. Alex was grinning ear to ear and feeling like he'd just won a prize for bravery. Mack hustled up the sidewalk and joined him on the porch.

"You crazy son of a bitch! You wouldn't have gotten away with that stunt in Iraq."
Alex smiled and took a gloating bite of his apple.

"When you're finished with your victory feast, do you mind calling DD? She'll want to know everything's ok."

The call was quick, and in a moment, DD opened the door. As disheveled as she was, Mac still took note of her nice legs beneath her robe. When he looked her in the eyes, she appeared to be angry, scared, yet glad to see them. Even without makeup, she was beautiful.

When she started to tell the story of how she got the email, Mac came back to reality. This was getting serious. A threat had come from someone whom they knew had a history of killing. In turn, she allowed each man to read the email.

"Wow!" said Alex. "I never thought these guys would come after a woman."

"These guys are slimeballs," said Mac. "They want what they want, regardless of who it is. Man, woman, it makes no difference to them. Their motivation is greed. DD, how are you holding up?"

"Better, now that you're both here," she said, trying to sound brave. She was scared, and they knew it.

Back to the matter at hand, Mac wanted to keep this conversation moving, but he wanted to do it in a safer location.

"Do you have a room in the middle of the house that doesn't have windows?" he asked, glancing around the room.

She thought for a moment, noticing that he was already locking the front door and looking out the window.

"What about the basement?" asked DD.

"That'll do. I don't like being in a basement with only one way out, but these windows leave us too vulnerable."

Before they knew it, all three were in the basement, but Mac wouldn't take his eyes off the door. He was being vigilant, and Alex knew that Mac's situational awareness was much more honed than his own. All these measures had value, but Alex was tired of it. It was Alex who broke the silence.

"DD, I'm sorry about the threat. To be honest, I told Juan the same thing. I told him I was sorry he got beat up and threatened. My being sorry wasn't enough. I'm tired of this defensive bullshit!" As Alex spoke, his sense of indignation was mounting. He continued, "I think it's time we rattle their cage for once. Let's find out who this is and take the fight to them."

"Alex, I don't like defense any more than you do. At this point, now we have an email that proves a threat. It's not how I wanna play it, but do we need to stop and just call the police?" asked Mac.

Unexpectedly, it was DD who spoke first. "Mac, they killed Juan. They threatened me, and I'm the one hiding in my house because of it. I'm in this as deep as either one of you. If this is as big as I think it is, they probably have people on their payroll with the PD as well. The police may actually make things worse."

"DD, you said what I was thinking," said Alex. "I do have one friend that works there in the department. I talked to him this morning on my drive over here. He said several of the high-ranking officers at the PD were on the take. He's willing to report it, but he doesn't know who he can trust. If he works there and can't trust them, how can we?"

"I can live with that," said Mac. "As we get closer to Tuesday, I expect things will get hotter."
Alex and DD both nodded and waited for Mac to continue.

"The only way we'll survive this is if we know more than we know today. We have to find out who's behind all of this. I agree with Alex. We have to go on the offensive."

They were all in agreement and started to talk about how they would find whoever was behind this. In the end, it was decided that Alex would work with Mark due to his extensive knowledge of the local players in the construction business. They were going to talk to as many contractors and subcontractors as they could. Hopefully, they could make enough inquiries that they might get lucky. Knowing it was a Friday, they only had part of the day left before the weekend. They would have to catch folks on the job sites over the next several hours if they wanted to get anything accomplished.

Alex concluded by saying, "Mac, I'll go with Mark. Between the two of us, we know most of the folks in town.

Hopefully, someone will be willing to give us something, but we've got to get started. It'll take time to drive to different job sites. Why don't you stay and make sure DD is safe?"

"Here is no good. We know from the email that they have her address. What we really need to do is move around. It's possible nobody knows that I'm working with you yet. I can keep busy today running errands. In the meantime, we can figure out where she'll stay this weekend."

"Alex, you go ahead and get started with Mark. I need to shower, get dressed and pack enough clothes to get me through Tuesday," said DD.

They all agreed, and soon Alex left the house. Once in his car, he called Mark who was more than willing to go with him to speak to other crews he had worked with in the past.

Back up in the main portion of the house, Mac was pacing. He looked out the front windows followed by looking out the back windows. He checked the sides of the house as well. In the small of his back, he was comforted to feel his Springfield Armory .45 nestled against his back.

"Do what you gotta do. I'll keep watch."

With that, she headed to her bedroom. He couldn't help but admire her courage. He knew she was scared, yet she wouldn't back down. Rather, she seemed to be emboldened in the face of the present circumstance. He knew he was there for a serious reason, and that she'd just lost her boyfriend. Regardless, he felt drawn to her, even longed for her. He had only felt this way once before.

CHAPTER 9

The Range

In about forty-five minutes, DD emerged from her bedroom. Gone was the robe and untidy look. Now, she was smartly dressed in practical, comfortable clothes. She was wearing hiking boots, a pair of black denim jeans and a peach, Polo style shirt. Her hair was pulled back into a ponytail, which brightened her face. Mac was somewhat self-conscious. His worn-out work boots, blue jeans and Carhartt T-shirt were normally comfortable. In this moment, he felt conspicuously underdressed. She was carrying two, medium-sized bags which she had packed for the weekend.

"What next?" she said inquisitively.

"Alex told me you have a gun."

"I do."

"Do you have a concealment license?"

"I do."

"Ammo?"

"Yes, it's loaded with hollow points, but I also have two boxes of plinking rounds."

He smirked and looked at the floor to conceal it. He had already gotten her to say "I do" twice. He tried not to let her see that he was pleased with himself. He made himself busy and continued.

"Perfect. When's the last time you went to the range?"

She could tell where he was going with this.

"It's been about a month," she said, knowing it had been over a year since she had practiced.

"It's been a while for me. Given the circumstances, I'd feel better if I brushed up a little bit. Wanna go to the range?"

"It beats standing around here. Since they know where I live, I feel like they're watching me, almost like a tiger in a zoo."

"Okay, let's take my truck," Mac said, as he picked up her bags.

He checked the window and, when he felt it was safe, walked briskly to the vehicle. He tossed her bags in the back and climbed in. She locked the front door of the house and followed him to the truck. Both were hyper-alert and scanning for anything out of the ordinary. Mac had felt this way many times overseas; it made him a little edgy. For DD, however, it was a new and nauseating feeling. She clutched her stomach as they drove away.

An hour later, they were surrounded by spent brass casings at their feet. They had each gone through two boxes of target ammunition. As DD finished her last magazine, Mac placed his left hand on her right shoulder. To her, it felt firm and strong.

"You're pretty good at this." He was looking down range at her target.

"You should see me with a rifle," she said, smiling. She was quite happy with her performance, and he was pleased that she could handle her weapon well. Once he had evaluated the group on her target, he continued,

"I'll sweep up the brass if you'll gather our stuff." His voice boomed as they were still on a hot range. Others were still firing, so they kept their earplugs in place. She nodded and started to gather their belongings. In just a few minutes, he had policed their area for brass. When he felt like the area was clean enough, he pointed to the door of the range.

"How was it today, folks?" asked the man behind the counter in the gun shop.

"Excellent!" said Mac. "This is my first time here, and I really like your setup."

"Thanks. We've been trying to make improvements to get more people in here. We just added a coffee and snack bar in the corner of the shop. You're welcome to stay a while if you'd like."

"DD?"

"That sounds good; it's been a long day already and I'm gettin' hungry."

"Snack bar it is."

Five minutes later, they were seated at a small corner table. Mac had ordered coffee and a pastry. DD had a bottle of water and an oversized pretzel with cheese. Once settled, it was DD who struck up a conversation.

"Mac, I'm sorry we dragged you into this."

"You're kidding, right? This is the way I see it: I was at work, and a bunch of lowlife thugs jumped me and your boyfriend. Well...me, Eli and your boyfriend. They dragged me into this, not you."

"But you were an innocent bystander that got caught up in our mess."

"Maybe. Regardless, you and Alex were not the instigators. This has nothing to do with you. It's got everything to do with the bad guys."

He wasn't expecting her reaction to that statement and was startled at her sharp, cutting tone.

"What do you mean it has nothing to do with me? It was my boyfriend that was killed and the company I work for that they're trying to cripple. And it's ME that they threatened this morning!" she declared, glaring at him defiantly.

"Whoa, whoa, whoa! Sorry if I hit a sore spot. I wasn't careful with my words. All I meant was that my motivation for being part of this is that I was attacked. I never intended to imply this wasn't about you. Only that my involvement comes solely from getting my butt kicked and watching a man die."

During these brief moments, she came to the understanding that it was never going to be the same for them. Her pain came from the loss of her boyfriend, and her fear came from the threats against her. Mac had been in a fight and lost. Although their reasons were different and, in her mind, her reasons were more important, she realized Mac hadn't meant any harm.

"Mac, I'm sorry. I think Juan's death and that email this morning really have me screwed up. I'm trying to keep a clear head, but sometimes I want to cry, and sometimes I want to choke the shit out of someone."

"Truce?"

"Truce," she agreed.

Once the awkwardness passed, she continued, "Let's change the subject. Tell me about you. Where is Mighty Mac from?"

Over the course of the next hour, they sipped their drinks and had a sincere conversation. In the background, they could hear the *pops* and *cracks* of firearms on the range, but neither one seemed to notice as they were beginning to enjoy each other's company. They shared stories which made them both laugh and weep. When they walked out of the gun store, they had begun to knit their hearts as friends.

Back in the truck, DD looked over at Mac and said, "Thank you for that. Shooting was a great distraction."

"Of course. I have three favorite things: shooting guns, coffee and having a conversation with a beautiful woman."

He almost choked. He wasn't supposed to say that last part. He knew that he had gone too far. Her head snapped left at the "beautiful woman" part. She looked him up and down from the passenger seat as she tried to figure out what he meant by that. She was still grieving Juan and couldn't even think about moving on. Her loss was too fresh. Mac awkwardly pretended he hadn't said anything unusual. As calmly as he could, he pulled out of the parking lot and started down the street. She didn't know what to say, so she said nothing. The awkwardness hung in the air between them for what seemed like an eternity.

CHAPTER 10

Full-Court Press

"Do you think we have enough?" asked Mark.
Alejandro looked down at their basket stacked with several cases of beer and bottles of bourbon. In his mind, this was currency he would leverage for information. Their biggest problem wasn't the booze, it was that they only had a few hours left before the job sites started shutting down for the weekend. Many of these crews left early on Fridays, and Alex wanted to make sure he talked to as many people as possible.

"It's enough. But we gotta get going if we're gonna make it to several sites," Alex responded.
Over the next few minutes, they paid the cashier, put the booze in the back seat of Alex's truck and headed for the first stop. As they pulled up to the first job site, they saw some familiar faces. Over the years, Mark and Alex had worked with many of these guys.

"Hola, amigos!" said a smiling, weathered old man.
"Que pasa, Abuelo," said Alex.

Mark, the old man and Alex exchanged handshakes and smiles. At one time or another, everyone had worked for the old man, affectionately known by his crew as "Grandpa." He had spent a lifetime working on projects. This meant that he had a lifetime of men coming through and working with him. After the pleasantries were exchanged, it was Mark who spoke first.

"Abuelo, do you remember Juan?"

"Juan Marc? Si. I know Juan."

"He was killed several days ago. Now Alex and DD are being threatened."

"Juan is dead!? He was a good boy. That's crazy. What's going on?"

Alex and Mark spent the next several minutes explaining the recent events. When everything was done, they looked at the old man, hoping for information.

"I'm sorry, amigos. I don't know anything, but I will keep my eyes and ears open."

"Gracias, Abuelo. It's always good to see your smiling face. Ask one of your men to walk to the truck with us. I have something for you," said Alex.

Grandpa waved for a young man to follow them to the truck. Alex grabbed a case of beer and handed it to him. The young man's eyes grew wide.

"Thank you, sir."

"Alex, Mark, this is Matt. He's young, but he's very strong," said Abuelo.

"Matt, this is for you and your crew. Maybe grandpa will let you off a little early today," said Alex with a smile.

Matt looked at Abuelo, who gave him a nod. The young man trotted off to tell the rest of the guys.

"And for you," Mark handed the old man a bottle of bourbon.

"Muchas gracias. Vaya con Dios," he said, smiling and giving them hearty handshakes as they climbed in the truck to go to the next job site.

"Where to next?" asked Mark.

"Let's see if we can get to Hank and his boys. Then, if we have time, I'd like to see David, the landscaper. He's always in on new developments. After that, Evan the bricklayer. He's got his hands in everything. If we have any time left, we may see what Lenny is hearing."

"Okay, Hank it is," said Mark in agreement.

The rest of the afternoon, Alex and Mark replayed the same scenario over and over. As the day wore on, they began to get tired and somewhat discouraged. It seemed that nobody had any information. And, after they had told the story of Juan's death several times, they were sick of it. What seemed like a good idea at the beginning of the day now felt hollow and hopeless.

"Mark, I don't think we accomplished anything afternoon."

"It sure feels that way. But we've met with dozens of guys today. I can't help but think someone knows something. Maybe they're scared," Mark said, staring out the passenger side window.

"Let's see what Lenny knows."

In a few moments, Alex was on the phone with Lenny. Lenny had wanted to meet in person, so they chose a parking lot at a local grocery store. Fifteen minutes later, their cars were side-by-side in a big, box store parking lot.

"Hey Lenny, what's the word?" said Mark.

"I'm glad you guys are here. I didn't want to talk on the phone."

"What's up?" said Alex, having to elevate his voice to speak across Mark.

"The word on the street is that there are two guys going from site to site giving out booze and asking lots of questions. Is that you guys?" asked Lenny.

"Yeah man, that's us," said Mark.

"Well, you're getting a lot of attention. When you go to sites telling stories of murder and asking who's responsible, it's like raising a billboard at rush hour."

"Lenny, you know we can't go to the cops. This is the only way we know to get information," said Alex.

"I get why you're doing it, but you're putting a target on your own backs."

Mark thought for a moment and then replied, "That's even better. Maybe it'll flush them out. I didn't think of it before, but them coming after us is probably the quickest way to get to them."

"Yeah, man, but it also leaves us vulnerable," Alex said, still thinking about it. "And what about DD?"
Lenny continued to listen as Mark talked to Alex.

"Look, DD can stay with me and Kathy tonight. You and Mac can take care of yourselves as long as you see it coming. To be honest, today I thought we were looking for information. The truth is, we may have poked the bear. From here on, we have to be ready for anything. As a matter of fact, I'm thinking of sending Kathy out of town."

"You have your gun, right?"

"Always, but I'd like to get home and get my hands on my 5.56."

Lenny jumped in, "Good idea. At this point, anything can happen. I gotta get back. I'll let you guys know if I hear anything else."

They exchanged their goodbyes, and Lenny drove away. The two sat silently for a few moments, considering their next steps. Neither one of them expected what happened next. Alex's phone rang, and when he looked down at the caller ID, it read "Mac." He swiped to answer.

"Alex, this is Mac. Are you still with Mark?"

"Yeah, he's here with me. We were able to visit several sites, and we just met with Lenny."

"Hey, man, I just got a call from Eli. He wants to talk to me, you and DD. He said just us three. You don't have me on speakerphone, do you?"

"No, Mark can't hear, just me," he said looking over at Mark.

"I'll step out and call Kathy."

Mac continued, "Okay, gimme a sec, I'm gonna try to put us on a three-way call."

Seconds later, Mac said, "Alex, do I still have you?"

"I'm here."

"Eli, can you hear us?" asked Mac.

"I can," said the strong, confident voice of Eli.

"Okay, it sounds like everyone is here. Eli, go ahead."

"Mac, DD, Alex, thank you for taking the time to speak with me. I need to tell you something. Sometimes..." he hesitated for a moment, "I know things. Sometimes, things just come to me."

The three were puzzled and wondered where this was going. They all respected Eli because of his willingness to fight for Juan, but they were trying to figure out what this was about when Mac replied to Eli.

"Eli, I've known you the longest. You've always been a good guy that seems to have a knack for being in the right place at the right time. I watched you when you helped Juan. All of us respect you for what you did that day. Go ahead and speak your mind."

After a brief pause, Eli continued:

You three have been chosen for such a time as this to defeat wickedness in our city. The Madison Complex will usher in a new era of prosperity for this community. Whether that prosperity comes to wicked men or to godly men is up to you. You have been chosen because local authorities have sided with wickedness. You are being raised up to fight for the soul of the next generation in this region. There will be a cost. Blood will be spilled. The outcome remains to be seen.

They all seemed a little lost while trying to sort out what had just been said. Words like "wicked" and "godly." None of them felt like they fit into either one of these camps. "Chosen." What was that supposed to mean? And "spilled blood" sounded threatening. These words were all swirling in their minds. It all seemed so dark and ominous.

It was DD who was able to collect her thoughts enough to ask a question.

"All due respect Eli, what are you talking about?"

"I cannot add to, change or interpret the message," said Eli. He sounded firm yet empathetic.

"Eli, what are you trying to say?" asked Alex.

"My part is to deliver the message. The rest is up to you. I must go now. Please know, I wish you all well. Goodbye, my friends."

They realized that he was now off the call. Down deep, each one of them knew something had just happened. They didn't know what, but they knew things had just changed.

"Well, that's not what I expected," Mac said.

"I don't get it," said Alex, still pondering what just happened.

"Did he just give us permission to go after these guys?" asked DD.

"I can't tell if he was giving us permission or a commission. It sounded to me like we just got our orders," said Mac.

They thought about it for several moments before Alex replied.

"Maybe it was both," he said, still trying to figure the whole thing out.

They were still in a funk when they decided that they needed to make arrangements for tonight. Alex looked out the window of his truck and waved for Mark to rejoin them. Once in the truck, he put Mac and DD on speakerphone. It took about five minutes, but soon they had a plan. Mac would take DD to Mark and Kathy's house for the night. Her previous concerns about having private time with Juan had evaporated with his death. The last thing she wanted now was to be alone. The thought of being with Kathy and Mark was comforting. Alex would meet Mac at his house to borrow one of his guns. After that, Alex would go back to his office and sleep on a cot in the back room. He felt safer there because the yard was surrounded by an 8-foot-tall, chain-link fence with privacy slats. In his estimation, he would know if anyone came in the yard. Mac said he felt safest at home. Being ex-military, he had stowed away several firearms and quite a bit of ammunition. He had cameras and motion detectors that would alert him to anyone on his premises. Once the arrangements had been made, they hung up and began to work their various plans.

None of the three who heard Eli could shake what he said. Each of them, in their own way, was trying to reason out and understand his words. Instinctively, each one knew that something had come alive down deep in their hearts: something powerful, something reverent, something dangerous.

CHAPTER 11

Dance with the Devil

She was stressed. It was Friday night, and Stacy had spent the whole day hustling to make sure the arrangements were perfect for Mr. Masters' party. He wanted an intimate affair, so it was to be hosted in his office, which was more than large enough for the twenty or so people invited. She set up the catering, DJ, and booze. The DJ had a small booth with additional lighting, which would help set the mood. Masters had also invited her, which she thought was unusual. Because it was her boss, and he didn't take "no" from any of his employees, she felt like she had to attend. She was thinking it wouldn't be a terrible way to spend her Friday night. After all, she was responsible for the arrangements; she could be there to make sure everything was to his liking.

She gave a lot of thought about what she would wear. Masters said it was a group of family friends from the East Coast that would be coming.

Was it business or family? she wondered.

Eventually, she settled on a red top and black skirt. Black stockings and black leather shoes would complete the look. She made sure her long, blonde hair looked perfect and did her best to get her makeup just right. She looked great, and she knew it. Secretly, she was hoping to meet some rich guy. Although Mr. Masters was kind of a jerk, she did like the money and power he exuded. She thought she might like a man like that.

She arrived an hour early to make sure everything was in order. After a few finishing touches, guests started to arrive. Mr. Masters had texted that he would be a few minutes late and asked her to make sure everyone was properly welcomed. When the first trio of men arrived, they looked like the typical businessmen she had seen doing business with Mr. Masters. She made sure they had drinks and hors d'oeuvres and asked the DJ to start playing music. She was proud of herself and felt like she was on her way to a successful evening.

The next group was very different. They gave her pause. She greeted them with the same, perky welcome, but she understood that these guys were unlike ordinary businessmen. The leader of the group, although well-dressed, was quite rough. His words were profane, he was boisterous and he had no shame in eyeing her like a piece of meat. The other men with him also dressed in suits, but they were obviously subservient to him. It reminded her of movies she'd seen where the lead gangster had thugs as bodyguards. These men didn't say much. They just stayed close to him and looked hyper-vigilant. Lastly, in this group were three young girls that looked between eighteen and twenty years old. They were dressed in extremely short skirts and showed way too much breast.

They look slutty, she thought.

A few moments later, she concluded that these young ladies were not friends or family; rather they worked for the boisterous man. Regardless, she did her best to make sure everyone had drinks and felt welcome. She smiled pleasantly but secretly hoped Mr. Masters would arrive soon.

A couple of other businessmen arrived, each one by himself. Stacy couldn't help but notice it was only her and the three other women. She continued to get more and more uncomfortable. The group of thugs continued to drink and get louder and more obnoxious. It wasn't long before the businessmen even started to cast uncomfortable glances at the raucous group. She caught herself standing next to the DJ booth being a little standoffish and noticed she was wringing her hands. Her stress level was palpable.

"Hey baby," said the leader of the pack, getting her attention.

She had hoped they would have talked among themselves, but now that he had called to her, she felt obligated to respond.

"Yes mister...I'm sorry, I didn't catch your name?"

"Rico. Rico James."

"How may I help you, Mr. James?"

"First, call me Rico. Mr. Masters and I are working on a big deal. What is your association with him? Girlfriend perhaps?"

"No, sir. I work for Mr. Masters as his receptionist."

"Oh, I see. This makes me very happy. If you're not his woman, then you can party with us."

At this suggestion, a chill ran down her spine and a wave of nausea gripped her stomach. She didn't want anything to do with this man. At the same time, she didn't want to offend Mr. Masters, so she delicately tried to brush him off.

She smiled and replied, "Thank you for the offer; however, it's important for me to see to the needs of all of the guests," as she motioned to other businessmen in the room.

He glanced around the room. It was the first time he seemed to notice anyone outside of his own entourage.

"Miss, what is your name?"

"Stacy," unwilling to give her last name.

"Miss Stacy, I don't think you understand the nature of our arrangement. Mr. Masters is hosting this party for me. These "others" that you refer to are only here to add respectability to our business deal. They're local men that my family and I may choose to do business with. I, however, am from a well-established family on the East Coast. Do you know what I mean by this?" he said with an imposing glare.

"I... I think I do," she said, feeling more and more overwhelmed. His body language was menacing. She sensed his last comments were thinly veiled threats.

Just when she thought things were about to go bad, Mr. Masters appeared, seemingly from nowhere. He stuck out his hand towards Rico and started to speak boldly. This jolted both Rico and Stacy out of their dark moment.

"Welcome, Rico. Welcome to you and your associates."

"Thank you for having us, Masters. Miss Stacy here has taken good care of us," he said, still ogling her.

"I would expect nothing less," he said to Rico, and then turned to Stacy. "Stacy, be a dear and ask the DJ to turn the music down. I can barely hear myself speak."
She nodded and headed for the DJ booth. It felt more like a retreat than an assignment. There was little relief because they were all still in such close quarters. In a

moment, the DJ had the sound turned down. Mr. Masters looked over at her and nodded.

Over the next hour, Mr. Masters ensured that all his guests had eaten well and had generous amounts of liquor. One by one, he introduced each businessman to Rico. Stacy watched as each man seemed to be tentative, yet willing to meet with him. The whole thing seemed forced. Each of them tried to hide it, but she could tell by their body language that Rico and his goons intimidated them. On the other hand, the three young ladies never moved from their spot on the couch. Not one of the businessmen even dared look in the direction of the beauties. She understood this was more of a business meeting, in that Rico James was in town to establish his presence. He was meeting with the players to let them know what he expected of them. As each one of these men met with him, Masters would stand by their side as if presenting each man for Rico's approval. Once each meeting was complete, the businessman was not allowed to stay at the party; rather, each one was escorted to the door, politely thanked by Masters, and for all practical purposes, dismissed.

After some time, all the businessmen had gone, and the tone of the evening changed dramatically.

"Mr. Masters, now that business is done, I'm ready to party!" bellowed Rico.

"As you wish," Masters replied. "DJ! Dance music and lights!" he commanded.

Stacy knew to dim the office lights so they would not take away from the effect of the DJ lights. When she did, the whole place seemed different. It was dark, with spinning lights of red and blue. The steady beat of the high-energy music was pounding in her ears. In a moment, the men in Rico's entourage had pulled out multicolored pills and a bag of cocaine. Masters and Rico were the first to roll up hundred-dollar bills and snort lines. After that, Rico demanded that the three young girls do the same. They started taking pills and washing them down with whatever booze they had close by.

In the middle of this, Stacy wanted to find the closest exit. Her nausea had returned, and she was trying to think of excuses to give Masters so she could leave. She looked for an opening and looked to respectfully pull him aside. When the moment came, she spoke up.

"Mr. Masters, it looks like your business is through. I'll excuse myself so you and your friends can enjoy the rest of your evening."

His response left her reeling. "Nonsense, you'll stay and party with us. Besides, Mr. James is quite fond of you."

She felt trapped. She looked at Masters as if to protest. Masters' return glare made it clear that she must stay.

She knew the night would not end well. She looked at him and submissively nodded in agreement. He loved having power over her. She couldn't think of anything else to do, so she tried to hide her sense of desperation. Still, she wasn't prepared for what happened next.

"Masters, you've been an excellent host. I see that my new friend, Stacy, is going to stay for a while," he said, eyeing her legs.

His piercing, shameless gaze at her legs made her even more queasy, so she stepped behind a couch in a vain attempt to hide them. It was the same couch where the three young ladies were sitting. She tried to ignore what was going on as she swirled the ice in her glass and took a long drink.

"I would like to repay your hospitality. My father and I have arranged for you to sample some of our finest products."

At first, Stacy thought he meant drugs, but then he motioned to the three girls.

Were these girls prostitutes?

No, she concluded that these girls were owned by Rico. Stacy was terrified for them. They looked scared, but all three stood up obediently. Masters could only smile and nod at the gifts he was being offered.

"Ladies, smile, dance, and turn around. We want to see which one of you Mr. Masters chooses," commanded Rico.

Stacy watched as each girl began to move with the music while they rotated on display. She was horrified. She saw that each woman was both frightened and trying to be sexy, but not sexy because they were trying to entice a man they were attracted to. No, they manufactured their sexy moves because they would be punished if they didn't. The fear in their eyes was painful to watch and soon, her own fear began to grow.

Masters stood and approached the three. He moved them from between the couch and the coffee table to an open space in front of the DJ booth.

"Come where I can see you better, ladies," he insisted.

There was no resistance as they stepped into the center of the floor and continued to dance. Then, Masters looked at Rico as if he had a question.

"What if I like two of them, my friend?"

Rico turned his gaze to Stacy once more and replied to Masters, "You may have two, as long as Stacy will get up on the coffee table and dance for me and my men."

At that moment, Stacy thought she would vomit.

Not me, I'm not one of "these" girls, she thought. *Oh...God! No! How can I get out of this?*

"Of course, she would be happy to dance for you," he replied, motioning for Stacy to move to the table. Masters dismissed one of the women. He was happy with his selections. His eyes were greedy, almost ravenous, as he watched the two, scantily clad women diligently writhing in front of him. To Stacy, it looked as if the wolf had cornered his prey.

"Excellent! Enjoy the products," Rico sneered, now looking at Stacy expectantly.

Stacy instinctively knew she should not protest. Masters grabbed the two girls firmly by the arms and went into the next room. Now, Stacy was alone with Rico James and his goons. Her worst fears were coming to life.

"Men, help Miss Stacy on to the table," he said to his thugs with a devilish grin, "I want to see the goods." In a moment, two men lifted her onto the coffee table where she stood with her high heels wobbling. Next came Rico's command.

"Dance for me, my beautiful Stacy." She started to move and sway with the music. She understood now why the young ladies had danced and tried to look appealing. She knew if she didn't, things would get worse. She tried to fake a smile, and she started to move her hips.

Stacy cringed and swallowed the bile in her throat as she thought, *this must be what hell feels like.*

The next morning, she awoke on the office couch. Devastated, she felt shame, pain and fear. She quickly gathered her things and left the office in tears.

CHAPTER 12

Sister Talk

"Oh my gosh," DD said to herself as she rolled over and stretched. "Something smells great."

It was Saturday morning, and DD had slept well at her sister's house. It was always so peaceful and homey that it reminded her of her parent's home. As she became more lucid, she realized that smell was bacon and coffee. She assumed there would be eggs as well. She wasn't quite ready to get up because her mind was still racing from all of yesterday's events. In particular, she couldn't get the words that Eli had spoken out of her mind. She didn't understand them, but they gave her this unusual sense of peace. She knew she should be scared, but she wasn't. Not anymore. Even beyond peace, she felt a sense of boldness. She hadn't finished processing her thoughts when there came a quiet knock on the bedroom door.

"DD, are you awake?" came Kathy's voice. It was so familiar and comforting.

"I am. Come on in, Sis," she said, sitting up on the edge of the bed.

"I hope you slept well."

"I did. But what I really wanna know is what smells so good?"

"Coffee, bacon, and eggs. It's ready if you are."

"Oh, I'm ready. It smells so good."

With that, both sisters headed toward the kitchen.

It wasn't long before Kathy had served the meal. The first few minutes were quiet as they began to eat. The toasty warm eggs and bacon felt like a warm blanket on a cold day. Soon, Kathy began the conversation.

"You know, I'm really worried about you. Mark says these guys are some real crooks. After what happened to Juan, I just don't want you to get hurt."

"The last thing I want to do is get hurt."

"Remind me why you guys think it's a bad idea to go to the police."

"Alejandro has a friend in the PD. He says there are high-ranking people in the department that are corrupt. The fear is that working with the police may actually become an advantage for whoever is behind all this."

"All the same, I wish you could just hand this whole thing over to the authorities."

DD had been wanting to turn the conversation a different direction. After a couple more bites and a few sips of coffee, DD was able to talk about what was really on her mind.

"Kathy, I want to share something with you that happened yesterday. Mac and I got a call from his friend Eli. He wanted to speak to me, Mac and Alejandro. Mac called Alex and put us on a three-way call. Now, I want you to know that this man, Eli, Mac respects very much. Eli was the third person in the fight when Juan was killed." At this last statement, DD began to choke up, and tears began to well in her eyes. She gathered herself and continued, "He was in the fight and, unlike Mac, he didn't seem to feel the need for revenge. I don't know what to make of it, other than he clearly isn't a man of malice."

"Go on."

"Well, he kind of said something that's difficult to describe. I wish I had a recording of it because it was confusing, and, at the same time, it seemed..." She was looking for the right word. "Powerful...yes, powerful is the right word."

At this point, Kathy was intrigued, "What do you mean 'powerful'?"

"The words he used were powerful. The way he said it was even more powerful. His voice was forceful and tangible. I felt like I could reach out and grab what he was saying with both hands. It was solid and pure."

Kathy's next response was not what DD expected. She didn't seem surprised at all. DD had expected to be blown off, yet Kathy responded very differently.

"I've heard of something like this before. Do you feel okay sharing exactly what he said?"

"Well, I think I remember most of it. He said something to the effect of, we were chosen because the authorities were corrupt."

"What do you mean 'chosen'?"

"Something about having to fight for the community. Something about whether the community will be governed by wicked people or godly people. On some level, it seemed kind of churchy," continued DD.

"I see. It's almost as if there's a foreshadowing or foretelling of an ominous event. Did it scare you?"

"No, just the opposite. For me, on the inside, I felt stronger, or maybe bolder."

"What do you mean?"

"Well...When he was finished, I thought I could actually do it."

"Do what exactly?"

"I don't know. I just know I can do it. In my deepest parts, all my fears and hesitations were extinguished. It was refreshing... empowering."

"Okay, Sis. Let me get this straight. A man that none of us ever met showed up out of the blue and helped

Juan during a fight. This same man randomly called you guys and told you that you were called to defend the community against an unknown wickedness. He basically said you guys are supposed to 'fight the good fight,' and that you were chosen to do so."

"Yeah, you pretty much summed it up." Still, it sounded odd, but accurate, the way Kathy put it.

"In essence, you, Alejandro and Mac were told that you are ministers of justice."

"I wouldn't have used those words, but... yeah. I think that's right." For the first time, she felt like those were the words that captured what she was feeling inside. From that point on in the conversation, DD had a sense of peace. She still didn't understand what it all meant, but she was coming to grips with the whole, "ministers of justice" thing.

It wasn't long before they finished their breakfast. Both were sorry that the moment hadn't lasted longer, but DD couldn't help the deep sense of love and respect she had for her younger sister. She thought, proudly, that Kathy moved and spoke with grace and wisdom.

CHAPTER 13

The Plan

The tension was growing. They all knew Masters' deadline was just a few brief days away. It was Saturday afternoon, and Mark had called the trio together. They were all at the Just Plain Rocks office. DD, Mac and Alejandro sat around the table looking at a phone in the center of it. Soon, it rang, and Mark's voice came through loud and clear on the speaker. He took no time at all getting to the point.

"It looks like the beer and bourbon run paid off. Between last night and this morning, I received three or four texts from men from different job sites. It seems there is a common theme in their stories. Typically, a guy shows up in a suit and asks for volunteers for special projects. He usually waves some cash in front of the guys to get their attention and then leaves a phone number. He never gives his name; he only leaves the crew with a phone number."

"You're saying there's been a guy going to different job sites recruiting muscle?" asked Mac.

"That's exactly what I'm saying. But there's more. One foreman was really pissed when the guy recruited about six of his men. He was frustrated because he was having a hard time meeting his deadlines already, and then half his crew walks off the job site. The odd thing is, they came back the next day beat up, looking like they had been in a brawl."

"It could just be a coincidence," said Alex.

I don't think so. This foreman said the day of the walk off, he had a run-in with one of his more seasoned employees. In their argument, the guy made a comment about taking the day off for some extra cash. As he walked off, he pulled a phone number out of his pocket and started to dial someone. Within a few minutes of that call, he had five other guys that were seen leaving with him. Most of them came back the next day, asking for their jobs back. They told the foreman that the older man had come into some legal problems and wouldn't be back anytime soon.

Mark let the information sink in for a moment before continuing.

"Here's the kicker. It was the exact same day Juan was killed.

"Mark, all of this seems to fit. I mean, his story seems to make sense. It doesn't take too much of a leap to think that maybe the six guys were recruited by the man who left his phone number. Just to be clear, do you think all of this is legit?" asked DD.

"I can tell you the foreman was mad at his guys. He's got a motive. He doesn't want anybody poaching his employees like that again. But even though he has a motive, it doesn't make him a liar. My sense is that the story is legit, and it's our first real lead."

Alex spoke next, "Mark, I'm looking at my two partners here, and they're nodding in agreement that this means something. What do you think we should do next?"

"The guy I spoke with didn't have the phone number of our mystery man. But he told me there's a crew working on the East Side today, and their foreman has similar stories. I'm on my way to that site right now. My plan is to see if some of the guys still have the man's phone number. If I get that, then maybe we can use it to make contact."

"Mark, how long before you think you might know something?" asked Alejandro.

"I'll be there in ten minutes. It may take a little time to strike up a conversation and get the number. My guess is an hour, maybe less."

"Sounds good; we'll wait for your call," said Alex.

They said their goodbyes and hung up. It was Mac who spoke next.

"Guys, we need more than a phone number. We need a plan. What are we gonna say if we call this guy?"

"I'm glad you brought that up. I have some thoughts that I'd like to share with you guys," said DD.

"We're all ears," said Alex.

Over the next fifteen minutes, DD laid out the details of her plan. In the end, both men were cautious but willing to put it into action. It was simple, smart and, most of all, it was doable.

"DD, it could work. I'm in. Now, all we need is a phone number," said Mac.

A short time later, Mark called with the number. After a brief discussion, it was determined that Alex would be the one to make the call. They decided on Alex because it was Alex's attention the bad guys had been trying to get all along. And it was Alex who they would perceive as having the authority to withdraw the bid. It seemed to the three that the villains, whoever they were, would work best with him.

Alex typed the number Mark had given them into his phone. He worked the plan as they had agreed upon and, in less than five minutes, he hung up and looked at his friends.

"It's time to get ready. The trap is set."

CHAPTER 14

The Snare

It was early Sunday morning, and Mac was lying prone, looking through the Redfield scope on his Remington 700 XCR Tactical rifle. He was confident in his 300 Win Mag. He was in the loft of the Just Plain Rocks workshop. Although this industrial section of town was quiet on a Sunday morning, he didn't want to draw attention, so he was using a suppressor, which made his weapon look even more ominous. He had the gun propped up on a bag of cement, which put him at a comfortable height for shooting. He also liked knowing his AR 10 was by his side just in case he needed a faster rate of fire. On his left was Mark, whose military experience made him a natural fit to be the designated spotter.

Mark was prone as well, and he had his .40 caliber Sig holstered on his right hip. His AR 15 was close by in case he needed it. For now, he was Mac's eyes. He had his spotting scope set up on a small tripod. From this vantage point, they could see the front gate, parking spaces and the front office. He was calling out the wind and distances for Mac. Soon, things would get exciting.

Inside the office were DD and Alex. They had rehearsed their lines several times at this point, and each one hoped they would be convincing. Although he was a fighter, Alejandro had little experience with firearms other than at the range. The Glock 19 9mm he had tucked into the small of his back felt uncomfortable and heavy.

I'll have to get used to carrying this thing if this goes on much longer.

His favorite weapon was a boot knife that he had spent time honing to a razor's edge the night before. It had been his faithful back up for years. He'd only needed it a couple of times, but it had served him well.

DD was pacing and practicing her lines under her breath. This was her way of coping with the stress of the moment. She thought about the day before, talking to her sister about boldness. She tried to reclaim those feelings and gather her courage. She wore a flannel shirt that was untucked to make sure it was hanging low enough to conceal Crockett. In her mind, she wanted everything to be perfect. She ran through her lines one more time. Then she thought about her gun: cleaned, chambered and off safety. She was methodical in her thoughts.

"Alex, I'm ready to get this over with. How much longer?"

"They should be here anytime. I'm gettin' anxious, too."

Alex began to fiddle with his earpiece. "Mac, can you guys hear okay?"

"Loud and clear."

"I got a car headed our way about half a block out," stated Mark crisply.

At this, Mac used his scope to find the car. From here on, he had eyes on the target.

"DD, they're half a block out. Let's take our places in front of the window like we practiced so we can give'em a show."

DD nodded as she and Alex moved in front of the window and began to argue.

Lance was trying to observe everything as he neared the Just Plain Rocks entrance. He didn't like the fact that Masters had insisted he take two of Rico's goons with him. These men sat in the back seat watching everything but were primarily keeping an eye on him. Things were getting hot now, and both Rico and Masters were getting edgy. Lance preferred to work alone, or at least with guys that he personally selected. He considered it an insult that Dick and Rico thought he couldn't handle this. He slowed before making his turn into the business.

Well, they left the gate open just like they said they would.

As he turned into the property and drove through the gate, he noticed movement in the window of the main office. He could see a man and woman in a heated argument. Most people would have paused and waited for the argument to end. Lance, on the other hand, was somehow drawn to the spectacle of it. He and the two men parked and stepped out of the car. They could hear cussing, screaming and hatred spewing from the building. The two men stood at the car while Lance approached the front door. He couldn't help but smirk at the fight inside. He had wondered if it was the stress of his threat that was making her angry. He liked the power of intimidating people, and she was no exception. Without knocking, he opened the door and stepped in. In an instant, he realized the woman was out of control. She looked like a tornado, stomping around the room, yelling and making a scene.

"You sorry sack of shit! You're the one who got me into this! All over this stupid contract!" she screamed at Alex.

"Shut up! I told you I was going to pull the bid. I don't want you to get hurt," Alex acted as if he was trying to calm her down. "That's why I called this guy," he said, motioning to Lance.

"What in the hell is he going to do about anything?!"

"He's here to take the papers."

DD had an incredulous look as she screamed, "And what papers would those be!?"

Lance was still enjoying the show. These two were going at it, and he relished the thought of an actual fight. He hoped it would escalate.

"Look, I know how scared you are. So, I called this guy and told him we were giving up. I told him we'd sign anything. There's a form to fill out with the city to withdraw the application. I filled it out and signed it. Today is Sunday. Once I give this to them, the threat goes away. That's the deal," he said, nodding to Lance and hoping he would confirm his story.

"I hate to break up the party. It looks like fun, but Mr. Marquez is correct. My boss has agreed to accept the withdrawal form. We'll simply file it with the city tomorrow. By Tuesday, the bid will no longer be valid," he said, looking at DD.

"So, you work for the bastard that threatened me!" she shifted her aggression towards Lance.

Lance was loving this moment.

Just one more dig will push this bitch over the line, he thought.

"Honey... I AM the bastard that threatened you," he said coolly.

Just as he had hoped, she flipped out. Now she was cursing both men back and forth. She was yelling, screaming and waving her hands about. She suddenly rushed at Lance and started beating his chest. Lance grinned an evil grin and held her so that her punches had little effect. Alex reacted by grabbing her and pulling her away from him and standing between the two.

"DD, you're acting crazy! I'm trying to help you, and you won't shut up! Get out! Get the hell out of my office! Take a week off. I'll call you in a few days," Alex yelled.

"You sick bastards can have one another!" she said as she grabbed her purse violently and headed for the door. She got one last verbal jab in. "Both of you can go to hell!" She threw the back door open and exited in a flurry.

The men out front could hear the commotion and see the argument through the window. When the woman ran out the back door, the goons heard the door slam and simply looked at one another.

"She's none of our concern," said one man.

"Agreed."

Mac and Mark could see DD exit the back door of the office.

"She's all clear, Alex," Mark said into his mic.

Back inside the building, Alex was secretly hoping the ruse had worked. He studied Lance's body language. Satisfied that Lance had believed the scene, he deliberately and calmly stepped behind his desk. He motioned for Lance to have a seat. Lance still had that sick grin on his face.

"Mr. Marquez, do you have the document?"

"I do, um... I'm sorry about this whole thing. She wasn't supposed to be here this morning."

As he talked, Alex took the piece of paper in front of him and carefully folded it twice. He grabbed a letter-sized envelope and put the paper in it. Lance was watching his every move.

"She didn't bother me. In fact, I envy her passion. Women like that are beautiful to me," Lance declared smugly.

Alex thought, *what a dick.* But to Lance, he replied, "I think she's hot when she gets like that. If I get her angry, I get the best sex."

Lance smiled a wicked smile at this last statement. He and Alex continued to talk.

DD retreated to the bottom floor of the workshop. On the counter was her earpiece. She picked it up, placed it in her ear and started to listen to the conversation.

"By the way, what is your name?"

"Now, Mr. Marquez... there's no need for you to know that."

Things turned even colder as Alex continued, "My friend thought you looked like an angry accountant." He was hoping to provoke the man into making an error.

"Your friend screamed like a little girl," Lance intended to cut back at Alex.

Alex was already angry, but he wanted to keep this guy talking.

"One thing has always bothered me. How did you know Juan would be alone the first night? And how did you know where he was going the day you had him killed?"

Lance grinned his sinister grin. He couldn't help but enjoy his power over this man.

"Now, why would I reveal my sources to you?"

Alex's face drained of its cordiality. His entire countenance stiffened, and he was almost mechanical in his measured reply. It was time for Alex to reveal his play.

"Look over in the second story window of our workshop," Alejandro said, motioning to the window. "I have a very dear friend up there whom you've pissed off. He has a sniper rifle pointed at your head."

Lance shuddered as he realized he had been duped. He knew Rico's men couldn't help him.

He tried not to look alarmed as he replied, "If I give you the name of the man that sold out your friend, will you give me the document and allow me to leave?"

"No, I want more."

"And what would that be?"

"Three things: I want the name of the man who sold out Juan, and I want the name of the man you work for. Lastly, I want you to call your boss and tell him you have the document."

Lance looked nervously around the room. He was hoping for help from somewhere. Knowing there was a sniper watching him made him feel like he had no other options. On the other hand, he knew if he survived today, Masters would kill him. He finally decided to deal with the present danger first, then figure out what to do about Masters later.

The men by the car were getting anxious. They both thought this whole thing was taking way too long. It was supposed to be a quick document pick up. They started looking at each other questioningly.

Mark could see them fidgeting and wondered how long they would be patient. Mac had a clear shot at a known distance. He was focused like a laser on Lance's head. Because of this, he no longer needed Mark to spot for him. Mark had now assumed a firing position with his

AR 15, and he was confident he could take both men out quickly if necessary.

Below them in the same building, DD was listening to Alex and Lance's conversation. She wanted to know the answers to Alex's questions, too.

"I'll give you the name of the man that sold out your friend. I'll call my boss and tell him you've given me the document. But if I tell you his name, he'll kill me."

"I don't think you understand. If you even try to move out of that chair without giving me what I want, your brains will be splattered against the wall. It'll be a terrible mess, but I'm willing to clean it up if I have to. What will it be today? Do I get your information or your life?"

The trap was sprung. This time, Lance was the one that could not get away. He knew it, but he couldn't think of any other options. After a long silence, he relented and gave Alex what he wanted.

"The man was on Juan's crew. His name is Jerry. For five hundred dollars, he texted me when the crew was leaving the first day. The second day, the greedy bastard charged me seven hundred and fifty dollars to let me know that Juan was going to the hardware store."

Alex was visibly angered by this. One of Juan's own crew, a man Juan had been friends with for years, had sold him out. Alex's fist clenched. Jerry would pay for his betrayal.

In the workshop, DD started to weep. She couldn't believe Jerry would have sold out Juan for so little. Until now, she had considered Jerry a friend. She was devastated. Jerry, that worm of a man, had set Juan up.

Lance saw that Alex was pissed, so he kept talking, hoping for a way out of this mess.

"Richard Masters."

"What?" Alex didn't quite believe what he heard.

He'd already said it once so, *what the hell*, thought Lance. "I said Richard Masters, owner of Sandie's Foundations and the most prominent contractor in the region. I work for Dick. Although, once I leave here, I'll have to leave the area or be killed myself."

Alex had gotten what he wanted. But now that he knew who was behind everything, he wasn't sure what to do next.

Outside, the men became more anxious. They were getting a little spooked because things were taking so long. They looked at one another, silently asking if they should go in and check on the situation. They nodded as they both decided they would have to be patient. Much longer and they would have to find out what was happening.

Mac held his aim, but because he didn't know who Richard Masters was, he asked Mark in a whisper.

Mark replied as quietly as he could, "He's the big dog in town. Some say that he's with the Mafia."

"Shit!" Mac said, emphatically but quietly.

DD couldn't believe it. Richard Masters. They had done some work for him before. She couldn't figure out why Masters would care so much about a concrete bid. Her questions were soon answered. Lance could see that he had Alex's attention.

"You see, he has allegiances to an East Coast family. This family is trying to leverage big contracts on the Madison Complex for one of the sons in the family."

"You're telling me that Masters is in the hip pocket of gangsters?"

Lance simply nodded.

"That means, even if we kill you, me and mine are still in danger."

"The only way you and your crew survive is to back out of the bid."

"Then we're back to the final matter of our agreement. Call Masters and tell him you have the document."

"If you'll allow me to reach into my pocket, I'll get my phone and call him."

"Slowly! Any fast moves and my trigger-happy friend might squeeze one off."

DD was listening to all of this. Her sadness had evaporated. She was getting angrier by the moment. She was angry about Juan, Masters, and even this guy. She still didn't know his name, but she knew he had set up the crew that killed Juan and had threatened her. Something was building in her. A sense of righteous indignation. This thing was welling up deep inside her chest: an overwhelming rage about the injustice of it all. She lifted her shirt next to her hip and put her hand on Crockett as she eyed the back door of the office through the window.

Simultaneously, Lance was retrieving his phone. He hit the speed dial and put the phone to his ear.

"It's done, sir," Lance said, trying not to sound different than previous times. After listening for a moment to a response from the other person on the phone, he continued. "Yes, I have it in my hand. They looked scared. They won't be a problem anymore."

As he completed this last statement, he looked up at Alex, hoping it met his approval. He wanted to get out of this mess and get out of town before Masters found out about his betrayal. Alex made eye contact and nodded.

"I'll bring it by your office tomorrow morning, sir. Enjoy the rest of your weekend."
He ended the call and looked at Alex, hoping for some sort of goodwill. Alex gave him a look of guarded approval.

"Good enough? Are we finished here?"

"We are. Now, I'll ask you to stand up slowly and walk to the door."

"Of course." He was being sure none of his moves were quick or startling. To him, it seemed like it took forever to stand up and walk to the exit.

DD couldn't take it anymore. She felt like the man responsible for Juan's death was slipping away. She couldn't let it happen. She couldn't restrain herself any longer. With all her might, she exploded through the door of the workshop, with a thunderous clatter, and sprinted for the back door of the office.

The men out front heard the sound and started searching for what it might be.

Mac and Mark could only watch as it only took her a few seconds to cross the distance to the back of the office. She threw open the back door with speed and violence.

Inside the room, Alex was stunned and pivoted to see why the back door had burst open. Lance had already begun to open the front door, but he, too, was startled and turned to see the commotion. DD stood defiantly in the center of the office.

"No, sir!" she screamed at Lance. "No way you walk out of here. You killed Juan. You threatened to kill me. Today, I am the judge. Today, you die!"

Boom! Boom!

Two 9mm shots to his center mass came from Crockett in rapid flashes. Lance's eyes stared blankly into infinity as he crumbled to the floor.

The men in front heard the shots and headed for the door.

Schtwick! sounded Mac's suppressed rifle. The first man dropped.

Crack! Crack!

Mark had taken the other man out. Neither one of them had made it halfway to the office.

It was Mark who broke radio silence first. "Clear?"

No response.

"Is everyone ok?" he asked frantically.

"Um...yeah," came Alex's voice over the radio.

"Okay, we're coming down. Be there in a minute," Mac replied.

Mark and Mac came through the back door. Alex was helping DD sit down on the couch.

Mac spoke first. "What the hell happened? We were seconds from getting this done."

Alex looked at Mac, then DD. "I don't know. She just burst in, screamed at him and started firing."

When DD spoke, it wasn't the scared and trembling voice they expected. It was strong and unwavering.

"This man would have gotten away with murder if he walked out. I couldn't let that happen. Eli was right. If the police are corrupt, it must be us."

Now it was the men who were taken aback. They had not expected her to respond so calmly. The silence lingered in the air because no one knew what to say.

Alex's phone rang, shattering the silence.

"Hello." He listened to the person on the other end. "Yeah, everything's cool. We need to talk later. No need to come over now." He swiped his screen and hung up the phone. "That was Lenny. He'd gotten word about some unusual noises coming from this area. I told him we were fine," Alex explained to everyone.

Mark was the first one to speak up about the practical matters that were becoming obvious to everyone.

"Um...guys, what do we do with the bodies?" he said, hoping someone had a great answer. "Also, what happens when the goons don't make it back, and this guy doesn't show up with the document tomorrow?"

With that, there began a flurry of conversation and activity. They had work to do and a brief window in which to get it done.

CHAPTER 15

The Week Begins

As she pulled into the parking garage of the multistory building, the butterflies in Stacy's stomach turned into a tumultuous sea of nausea. She never wanted to go back into this building again. She hated Masters for allowing Friday night to happen. She knew the whole thing was no accident; on the contrary, she believed he had set the whole thing up. She felt like a piece of meat tossed to a ravenous wolf. But there was one other thing she couldn't get out of her mind. As vile and wicked as these men were, she couldn't help but think of their opposite. She had only met him once, but she knew he was different: compassionate, yet powerful. She had the entire weekend to think about what she was going to do. She walked in the building on a mission.

Stacy felt like a phony, but she was committed to continuing the charade as long she had to. She sat down at her desk and appeared to work as usual to not raise any red flags. When Masters arrived, she greeted him as always and pretended nothing was wrong. Masters was arrogant enough that he didn't even consider how she would feel about Friday night. He never once expressed concern for anything other than his daily business.

There it is.

She found Eli's contact information on the computer under Mr. Master's contacts. She pulled out her own phone, typed in the number and hit save. She would have to wait till later to call him.

* * *

Across town, Mac, DD and Alex were meeting in the freshly cleaned office. It was annoying because it still had a strong, nose burning stench of bleach.

"I don't know about you guys, but I didn't get any sleep last night," said Alex.

"I couldn't sleep either," said DD. "It wasn't so much what happened yesterday that kept me awake. It was more about making sure our preparations today were in order. My mind was racing because I was worried that I might miss something."

At this last statement, Alex and Mac simply nodded in agreement.

"Well, I figure sometime this morning, Masters will be calling," said Mac. "By the way, did we get to all of the employees last night?"

DD had the update, "I was able to get all but a few. Most of them were happy to have the day off. I told them you," she motioned to Alex, "had a family emergency back home. No one really questioned it, but a couple of the guys didn't want to lose a day of pay. No real pushback from them though. There were only a couple that I couldn't get through to. I figure one or two may show up to a job site or the gate here. Some will call and ask why we're closed."

"And Jerry?" asked Alex.

"I gave him some BS about his paycheck being messed up. He's supposed to be here about four p.m. to meet with me."

"That'll work. Mac, how about you?"

Well, I brought the drone out yesterday afternoon and took some pictures of the layout here. I spent the evening working out the best locations and angles for us to take. The problem is, we don't have enough help to cover such a large facility. When Mark found out that it was Mafia-related, he insisted on getting Kathy out of town. So, the plan is developed around it just being us three. I've also tried to anticipate other ways they might try to get in here beyond the front gate. We're vulnerable in several spots.

Mac pulled out pictures he had gotten from the drone and placed them on the table. Methodically, he started to review possible points of entry, firing lanes and locations of cover. He was explaining how, in each zone, they each would be able to shoot and move within their assigned location. After half an hour, each one understood their role. Each one understood that, if there were more than five or six guys, they would be easily overrun.

They all had a sense of foreboding. It seemed like too much. Once laid out, they realized that, even though it was their turf, they were outmatched. It was Alex who broke the silence.

Guys, this whole thing has been heavy. When I look at the plans and the details of what we're trying to do, my brain tells me we've gotten in way over our heads. I believe this to be true. On the other hand, for some reason, I can't let go of what Eli told us. His words come to mind even more powerfully than our present circumstance. It's his words that I think about when I'm in bed and can't sleep. I can look you both in the eye today without fear and say that I will not back down from this evil. I will not let this wickedness have place in my community. I will not allow them to control the future of this region.

Mac and DD couldn't help but respond to this. As he spoke about Eli, each of them surged with a sense of courage. When he spoke and said he would not allow wickedness to rule the future of this community, they felt bold and powerful. They became strong and capable. Most of all, they felt dangerous for good!

"Alex, I'm with you. They don't get to take another life. They don't get another day," said Mac. He was searching for more words because he wanted to go on, but it was DD who completed his thought.

"Today, we execute justice."

* * *

Masters started drinking early today. He once again stood with a glass of Jack Daniels in hand. He watched the ice glimmer as he gently swirled it in the glass. He walked over to the window and looked at the city. He took a long drink and thought about how well things were going. Once Lance arrived with the document, he would have

Rico off his back. In his mind, his new friend could continue to give him additional influence. Rico could go from a threat to a valuable asset. Masters' greed was rooted in the deepest recesses of his dark soul.

It's not like Lance to be this late, he thought, as he glanced at his watch. *Ten a.m. Where could he be?*

He stepped out to the lobby.

"Stacy, have you heard from Lance this morning?" She looked up and feigned the best smile she could. "No, sir. I haven't seen or heard from him today."

"Okay, if I don't hear from him soon, I'll call him myself."

As he went back into his office, her countenance fell. She hated being around him and was looking forward to her lunch hour when she intended to talk to Eli.

CHAPTER 16

Baiting the Hook

Back at Just Plain Rocks, DD had reentered the office building.

> It was just a couple of our guys from crew number three. They wondered why no one showed up to the job site this morning. When I told them I'd tried to call them yesterday, they looked a little sheepish. Neither one had bothered to check their messages. In the end, they seemed happy to take the day off. At this point, I think I've gotten in touch with everyone.

Just as Alex was about to respond, a phone rang. They all knew it was Lance's phone. Alex took a deep breath to calm his nerves before answering.

"Hello."

Masters was angered that it was a voice other than Lance's.

"Who in the hell is this?"

Alex was intentionally snarky with his reply, "Is this Richard 'The Dick' Masters?"

His jab worked. Masters was even more angry now.

"You sorry Motherf..."

"Whoa... Whoa... Whoa... Language," said Alex, intentionally cutting him off.

A slew of obscenities followed. Alex put his phone on mute and looked at the other two.

Alex couldn't help but grin as he told them, "Oh, he's really pissed!"

They nodded. All was going according to plan. Then, Alex remembered he needed to get back into character. He cut off Masters' rant once more.

"Hey... Hey... Hey... When you're done bitchin', I'll tell you what's going on."

After a few more expletives, Masters paused and demanded, "Tell me who you are, you coward!"

"Dick, I'm no coward. My name is Alejandro Marquez. My friends call me Alex. You may call me Mr. Marquez."

Another string of profanities followed.

The next thing Masters heard stunned him. It was Lance's voice, not so much talking to him, but rather, about him. Alex was holding his phone next to the speaker on his computer.

"...I said Richard Masters. Owner of Sandie's Foundations and the most prominent contractor in the region. I work for Dick... he has allegiances to an East Coast family. This family is trying to leverage big contracts on the Madison Complex for one of the sons in the family..."

Alex grinned at his audio splicing. He was confident this would set off Masters. He clicked pause on the computer and held the phone back to his ear.

Silence.

"You still there, Dick?" he asked condescendingly.

Bile rose up in Masters' throat. He was wondering what else Lance had told them. His mind was racing. He knew this information was a threat to not only himself but Rico and the family. From here on out, he would be more controlled with his responses. Ranting wouldn't give him what he wanted. He'd have to figure out what would appease Alex.

"I'm here. What do you want from me?"

"Funny you should ask," said Alex, oozing sarcasm. "It's quite simple, really... I want you dead."

"What the hell?"

"Hear me out."

"Why should I?"

"Cause, I have your boy down here in my workshop. By the way, what's his name?"

Feeling betrayed because of the recording, he was happy to throw him under the bus.

"His name is Lance."

"Okay... Well, Lance is tied to a chair and, after a little persuasion, including the loss of a couple of fingers, he started to sing like a canary. What you heard a moment ago is only a snippet of the recordings I have," exaggerated Alex.

"So what? You know that I'll kill you if you take that to the authorities. There is no 'win' for you, Alex."

"I told you to call me Mr. Marquez."

"You piece of shit!"

"Come on... say it..."

Masters was seething, and Alex knew it.

"Damn it! Fine! There is no 'win' for you, Mr. Marquez," he said loathingly.

"On the contrary, Lance has been quite forthcoming. He knows some important stuff, so he and I are in negotiations."

"What do you mean?"

"Well, he said you were a Dick and that you would turn on him. He said you would kill him if he stayed in town. I've offered him fifty thousand dollars, and I have a friend willing to fly him out of the country. He likes my offer much better than what you'll do to him."

"The bastard is a disloyal coward!"

"Dick, I said we were in negotiations. I didn't say the deal was done. I'd rather use him for bait. I think, if I keep him tied up in my workshop, it'll force you to come and kill him for fear that he'll keep talking."

Masters was trying to control his anger.

"Where are you going with this?"

It was time for this dance to stop. Alex wanted to be clear with his next message. He spoke slowly and carefully.

"At six p.m. today, the industrial park will be a ghost town. No one will be around to hear our business. I'll have Lance tied up on the bottom floor of my workshop. I'll move the audio files to a jump drive and put it in his suit pocket. If you want to come kill him and take the jump drive, I'll leave him there until six-thirty."

"How do I know you won't keep copies?"

"You won't know that for sure. You'll have to take my word for it."

"You'll forgive me if I don't believe you. After all, this whole thing sounds like a trap. How do I know you won't have the police waiting for me?"

"You're right, it's a trap. I'm personally gonna try to kill you. As far as the police being here, we crossed that bridge when we killed the two thugs you sent with Lance yesterday."

"You killed two of Rico's men? You'll answer to more powerful men than me."

Alex was proud of himself. Now he had a name.

Maybe Rico would like to hear the audio? Regardless, Lance will be available for you to kill at six. At six–thirty, I let him go and send him out of the country. I'll assume you didn't care enough to try and keep him from talking. My next move will be to track down the person that Rico reports to and get them the audio files. I'm sure they'd like to know how you've exposed their operation. I figure, at that point, you won't be able to run far enough to save yourself. It's your call.

"You expect me to walk right into your trap?"
"I've given you a choice: my trap or the East Coast Mafia," and he hung up the phone.
The hook was set.

CHAPTER 17

The Diner

"Yes?"

"Sir, are you Eli Seahur?"

Stacy had just pulled out of the parking garage at Sandie's Foundations. She was eager to call Eli as soon as possible. She really wanted to see this warm and kind gentleman face-to-face. She was hoping for lunch someplace where they could talk discreetly.

"That's me."

"Sir, you may not remember me, but I met you last week at Sandie's Foundations. I'm the receptionist for Mr. Masters."

"Yes, I remember you. Stacy, isn't it?"

"Yes, it is." She was grateful he remembered her.

"Does Richard want to talk?"

"Oh... I'm sorry for any confusion, but Mr. Masters doesn't know that I'm calling you. I have a personal matter that I would like to discuss. If it's not too much trouble, I'd like to meet."

In her mind, this sounded like a strange request, but to Eli, it was quite ordinary. People, even strangers, would often confide in him. It had happened so many times that he felt like it was his calling. He had no qualms about meeting her.

"Stacy, I'd be happy to meet with you. When and where is good for you?"

"There's a diner on Industrial and Second called April's. Do you know it?"

He chuckled as he responded, "Know it? I'm sitting in it."

"Oh... You're already eating? I'm so sorry to bother you."

"It's no bother. I just sat down. I'll ask the waitress to bring another setting."

"You're so kind. I'm close by, so it shouldn't take me long to get there.

A few minutes later, Stacy walked into the diner. Eli saw her enter and, with a genuine smile, he waved for her to come over. She waved back and headed for his booth. In a gentlemanly way, he stood up and extended his hand as she approached.

"Welcome, it's good to see you again."
He could tell by the look on her face that her heart was heavy. Despite this, she mustered a smile and thanked him for meeting with her. They sat down, and Stacy took

a long drink from the water that was in front of her. She set the glass back down on the table and began to speak.

"Thanks for meeting with me on such short notice. I hope I didn't mess up any plans you might have."

"No, not at all. I'm happy to have your company."

"Well... I have some things to say... But I'm not sure where to start..."

He put his hands up in a pausing motion, "We can get to those things in a moment. Let's take a minute to order and get some food on the way. Once she's taken our order, we can talk about whatever you'd like."

Stacy realized she had come across as anxious and harried. His words were calming and, now that she considered it, she was getting quite hungry. She was thankful for his suggestion.

"Great idea," she said as she picked up her menu.

After a few moments, the waitress approached them, and they both gave their orders. It made her feel better to know that the food was coming. Eli squeezed a lemon into his tea. After this, he stirred his drink and set his spoon down. When this ritual was completed, he was ready.

"What's on your mind?"

"I know this is awkward, but I feel like you're someone I can trust."

"Go on."

Over the next half hour, she told him her story. Painfully, she ended with the events of Friday night.

"I feel dirty. I feel ashamed. I don't know what to do. Sometimes, I just want to die, and sometimes I get so angry I want to kill that son of a bitch."
She felt bad for swearing in front of Eli. The look on her face belied her thoughts.

"I'm so sorry... I didn't mean to say that."

"Stacy, no worries. I'm not here to judge you. I'm here to listen."
His kindness was a relief to her. She could see by his demeanor that he honestly was not offended. What he said next was shocking.

"Richard Masters is a very wicked man."

"But I thought you two were friends."

"Childhood friends, yes. As adults, we've gone down separate paths. I don't approve of his actions, and he knows that." He gave her a moment to process what he had just said. He continued, "Your story only confirms what I already knew."

"If you knew what he was like, why didn't you go to the authorities?" she asked in a tone that was almost accusing.

"Do you think I didn't? I've been to the powers that be only to get blown off. On multiple occasions, I've had actual proof of wrongdoing. Still no help from them."

Her heart sank. She had hoped the authorities would do something if they knew what was going on.

"So, what do we do? What's the answer?"

At this question, Eli seemed to change. He sat up straighter as if he had called himself to attention. His facial expression firmed as if he personally was very determined. His voice was strong, and his voice began to penetrate her very soul.

"Stacy, in this matter, you have been wronged. Justice will be done. God, Himself, has raised up three people to confront this evil." His eyes were piercing her. "There will be a whirlwind tonight. His vengeance draws nigh."

As suddenly as this started, it stopped. Eli was back to his normal, gracious self.

"You see, Stacy, the Wheels of Justice are already in motion."

For what seemed like an eternity, they both sat silently. A couple of minutes later, the waitress came and collected their plates. Although Stacy protested, Eli took the check. It was one more unexpected act of kindness that endeared her to him.

Stacy looked at her watch and felt pressed for time.

"Oh my, I lost track of time, I have to get back to work," she said, gathering her purse.

"Stacy, I don't mean to be intrusive, but I don't think going back there today is a good idea. What if you called in and let him know something has come up, and you need the rest of the day off? I've got some errands to run; you can spend the afternoon with me."

She didn't want to go back, but she knew there'd be hell to pay if she didn't get back before her lunch hour was up. She shuddered to think what Masters would do or say to her.

"I wish I could, but I don't think it's a good idea," she said, hanging her head. She felt trapped.

"Dear God, release her from this wicked man's clutches," said Eli.

She was startled at his declaration. She started to think about it. She did like the idea of not being under Masters' thumb. She found herself daring to hope for a way out.

Masters was sitting behind his desk rather than staring out of his favorite window. He had been stressed out since the phone call with Alex a couple of hours before. It was nearing one p.m., and the day seemed to be getting away from him. He knew he had to call Rico, but that was the last thing he wanted to do. He expected the phone call to go badly and knew Rico would be in his office shortly thereafter. He was trying to think of ways to defuse the anger that was inevitable.

"First things first," he said aloud. "No witnesses."

Stacy was still reeling from Eli's previous statement when she was startled by her phone ringing. She looked at the name on the screen and knew it was Masters. Her hands trembled as she answered.

"Yes, Mr. Masters, I'll be back at the office in about ten minutes. Is there something you need before I arrive?" She was trying to be as accommodating as possible, hoping to keep his anger assuaged.

"Stacy... Something has come up that requires my immediate attention. It's of a personal nature, so I'm closing the office early today. Take the rest of the day off but be ready to go again tomorrow at eight a.m. sharp."
A wave of relief flowed through her body. It made her happy to know that today she didn't have to go back to the office and be with him. At least she didn't feel like she had to continue to serve the monster. Tears formed and slowly overwhelmed her eyes.

"Yes, sir. I have plenty to do this afternoon. I'll see you first thing in the morning," she said, trying not to change her tone, which might reveal her joy.

"And Stacy, do try to be on time tomorrow."

"Yes, sir. Eight, sharp. Goodbye," she said as she hung up. Her entire countenance changed. She tucked her phone back into her purse and said, "That was Mr. Masters. He told me to take the rest of the day off. He's never done that before. I'm so relieved that I don't have to go back in there today."

Eli was genuinely happy for her.

"Well then, the offer still stands. Would you like to run a few errands with me?"

"It would be my honor." She reached out and shook his hand almost as if they had become partners.

"Sounds great! I'll drive."

As they exited the building, she was trying to explain to him how she felt. She was searching for the right word.

"I just feel so... relieved. Maybe it's more like... there's a weight off my shoulders. Or maybe, a light just came on in a dark room." She was still struggling for a good description of her emotional state.

As they climbed in the truck, Eli looked over at her and asked, "Do you feel like you just got set free from a trap? Does it feel like you just escaped something ominous?"

"I didn't think of it that way, but yes, it is kind of liberating to know I don't have to go back today."

"Maybe you'll never have to go back. Maybe your time serving Masters is over. Maybe you have been released," he said powerfully.

"Released." Yes, that was the best word to describe this feeling of being liberated. She was thankful he had used that word. It seemed to resonate within her, which brought a new level of peace. Soon, Eli had pulled into traffic, and they were driving to their next destination.

CHAPTER 18

Masters on Point

Masters was sitting in Stacy's chair watching the front door, which was locked for the rest of the day. He didn't want Rico to wait when he arrived, so he was watching the door vigilantly. When Rico James and his men showed up, he would simply unlock the door, let them in and lock it behind them. He was on his third round of Jack Daniels and Coke and was already starting to appreciate its effects.

Masters could see through that glass door that Rico looked angry as he approached the office. Masters quickly stood, walked to the door and let them in. It wasn't long before the door was relocked, and they had all filed into Masters' office. Masters started to walk past the men to step behind his desk.

Crack!

Masters stumbled forward; his ribs landed awkwardly against his desk. He grabbed the back of his head where he felt the pain of the blow. When he turned around, he saw one of Rico's goons with brass knuckles on both fists. He could feel the gash in the back of his head start to bleed. He brought his hand back around to see what it looked like. It was covered in warm, red blood.

"What the hell!"

Rico replied, "You know, when you called and told me about Lance getting captured, I wanted to kick your ass. At the same time, I must respect my superiors, so I called them first. After I told them the story and explained how I'd already lost two men because of your incompetence, I received my instructions. First, I'm supposed to remind you that errors of this nature will not be tolerated. This is how I've chosen to remind you."

He reached in his pocket and handed Dick a handkerchief.

"Here, try this."

Masters took it and tried to clean the blood from his hand. It helped some, but his hand was still red. He folded the bloody material into a four-inch square and pressed it against the back of his head, hoping to stop the bleeding.

"Personally, I think I'm being lenient. I thought of removing a finger or scarring your face, but what can I say? I'm a nice guy. Second, I've been instructed to make sure Lance is neutralized, so he won't be able to talk anymore. It goes without saying that we must also have the audio files."

Rico's men were still leaning into Masters' personal space and they had him backed against the front part of his desk. Even holding pressure on the wound, he could feel the blood running down the back of his neck. It had started to soak into the collar of his shirt.

"In order to make sure Lance dies, and knowing we are walking into a trap, I'm going to put you out in front when we bust in on these guys. You'll be in the line of fire, Dick. Do you agree to take point on this, or do I have my guys kill you now?"

For the second time today, Masters was given a choice that he hated. The only thing he could think of was to buy time. Maybe, just maybe, if he lived through this, the family would trust him again and continue to support him.

"Rico, I'm willing to take point. If I do this, will you and your family continue to back me?"

Mr. James flashed an evil grin.

"If you live through this, and the mission is accomplished, maybe we'll talk about it."

Rico motioned for the men to back off. As they stepped back, Masters slipped behind his desk. Rico sat across from him and the men stationed themselves by the door. Once seated, he began to speak.

"I Googled the address and was able to find some satellite pictures of the property. I think we need to approach the location from multiple directions. I've got two other men I trust. How many do you have?" said Masters, trying to focus on gaining Rico's confidence.

"This goes down in just a couple of hours. I don't have time to bring anybody in from the East Coast. I've got these two, plus three more."

Masters was thinking out loud now, "You, plus your five, and me plus my two gives us nine, total."

Rico nodded, "The numbers are fine, but how do we keep the police away?"

Masters didn't respond. He simply picked up his phone and made a call.

"Hey Chief," he said. "Some friends and I have some work to do in the industrial park this afternoon. There may be some noise reported. I would appreciate some privacy."

Masters looked up at Rico while he was waiting for a response from the other end. Rico nodded his approval as Dick listened to the man on the phone.

"Thank you," said Masters into the phone. "Let's play golf soon. I'll bring the drinks."

He hung up the phone, quite proud of himself. He hoped his connections would make Rico realize that he was still valuable. It might just save his life.

"Dick, if you survive this, you may be worth keeping around," Rico sneered.

"Thank you, Mr. James. I think the next step is to gather the men and come up with a plan."

"I can have my men here in the next thirty minutes. They'll bring some additional firepower. I just want you to remember; it will be you and your two men going through the front gate."

"Understood."

"By the way, I'm very disappointed that it was you who let us in. I was looking forward to seeing Stacy."

"I thought you would have wanted privacy. I told her to take the day off."

"Humph... I wish she would've been here. I especially like her long legs. It would've made the next half-hour more interesting."

Still wishing to gain his approval, Masters replied, "If all goes well this afternoon, I'd be happy to arrange something with her this evening."

"Yes, please do. I like her... enthusiasm."

CHAPTER 19

The Cabin

"Well, this should do until everything blows over. At least you'll be safe," said Mark.

They looked at the cabin through the windshield of Mark's pickup truck. It looked nice enough: homey, rustic, clean and well-kept. And they were about 100 miles from town. There was little chance anyone would find them here. Kathy looked over at Mark and nodded in agreement, but she still did not have a peace about being here.

"It looks fine, honey. Let's get our suitcases in and get settled. We also need to take in the ice chests. I'll get everything into the fridge and start dinner around five."

Over the next ten minutes, several suitcases and two ice chests were carried into the cabin. It was comfortably furnished, and Kathy was pleased with the accommodations. She was already in the kitchen putting things away when Mark walked in carrying his last load.

His AR was slung over his left shoulder. He also had an ammo box in one hand and his pistol case in his other.

"Mark, thanks for taking such good care of me," she said, as he was putting down his weapons.
She stepped in and gave him a hug. She was thankful that she had a man she could trust. His tattooed arms made him look rough, but she knew the real Mark. He was a good man. He was strong and genuine in his concern for her wellbeing. He'd been a great husband. Since he'd gotten out of the military, he had been a highly sought-after employee amongst the contractors in the construction business.

His instincts told him to be alert, but his heart told him he was behind the lines and far away from the battle. Now that Kathy was safe, he couldn't help but think of how everything would go today. His mind went to his trio of friends. He was sure they were in harm's way.

Kathy could tell that his mind was elsewhere. She walked over to the refrigerator, pulled out a cold bottle of water and handed it to him. He was sitting at the kitchen table checking his firearms, so she sat down across from him. She didn't say a word at first; rather, she let him finish his methodical process. When he finished, he looked up at her and took a long draw of his water.

"Mark... why are you so anxious? Do you think we were followed?"

"No, not at all. I'm not even sure the bad guys know I exist. I watched our six the entire way up here. I don't think anyone would know where we are."

"Well, at least tell me what you're thinking."

"The truth is, Mac is the only one trained for this kind of stuff. Alex is good in a bar fight, and DD has proven that she's willing to kill if necessary, but that doesn't mean they're ready for this kind of violence. I'm worried about 'em."

"I'm scared for DD. I know she's decent with a pistol, but target practice isn't the same. I know you told me she killed that man, but even that's hard for me to picture."

"Kathy, DD was bold as a lion. But I keep thinking that we were in total control of that situation, and we had the element of surprise. This is completely different. They'll come with more people and from more angles. Mac is a badass with a rifle, but even he can only do so much."

Kathy's face was solemn. She knew Mark was right. She felt a little bit sick knowing that she was safe, and her sister was in danger. She didn't say another word to Mark, but she looked at him with a knowing smile as she picked up her phone and hit speed dial.

"Hey, DD, it's Kathy," as she put her phone on speaker.

Now Mark could hear the conversation as well.

"Hey, Sis, what's up?"

"We made it to the cabin. Mark's confident we weren't followed. So, all is safe here. I'm worried and I don't want anything to happen to you, or the others for that matter."

"Well...Things are already in motion. It's five minutes till four, and Jerry will be here soon. We're already committed."

"After you deal with Jerry, what time do you expect things to go down?"

"We told 'em six o'clock, but we're already on high alert. We don't want them to show up early and surprise us."

Mark had been listening this whole time. He was figuring in his mind how long it would take to get to them. At just over 100 miles, he could be there in an hour and a half. The trouble was, there were about ten miles of a bumpy dirt road he had to take slowly. The other matter was that the industrial park was on the opposite side of town, so there would be a substantial amount of traffic between five and six p.m. Mark did some quick figuring in his head.

"DD, I think I can be there in a couple of hours. I'd like to come help."

Kathy noticed that it was the first time Mark seemed enthusiastic all afternoon. He really wanted this. He wanted to be in the fight. No, it was more than that. He *needed* to be in the fight. She knew she had to let him go.

"Mark, get in your truck and go help these guys kick some mafia ass!"
It was the first-time all-day Mark had smiled. She could see that he was sincerely happy to go help his friends.

"Hell yeah!" said Mark, as he jumped up and leaned over to kiss her. "DD, I'll be there as soon as I can. It would be rude to start the party without me," he said jokingly.

"Com'on! The sooner the better."
DD was grateful they had help coming, and she was glad it was someone with combat experience.

"Hey guys, I hate to rain on our little parade, but Jerry is pulling up to the gate. I gotta go deal with him. Sis, I love you. Mark, see you soon."

"I love you too. Be safe. Bye, girl."

Kathy looked at Mark, "How can I help you get outta here?"
Mark was already gathering his guns and ammo. He had made sure his guns were loaded and ready to go in case he drove up and the scene was already hot. He grabbed the water bottle and handed it to Kathy.

"Kiss me and finish my water. I'd hate for it go to waste," he said smiling.

She kissed him and followed him out to his truck. In a few moments, he had his firearms in the vehicle. He hopped in and rolled down the window for one last goodbye. Kathy spoke first.

"Be safe, kick ass and know that I love you!"

"I will, and I love you, too!"

She raised her water as if to say, "cheers" as he drove away. As she turned to walk in the cabin, she took a sip from the bottle. Over the next few hours, she would have her phone next to her every moment, hoping for a call. She knew Mark was headed for danger, but she couldn't have felt more right about it. For the first time today, she was at peace.

CHAPTER 20

Jerry the Worm

DD hung up the phone and looked at her two friends. They had been listening to her side of the call between her and her sister. They had also been monitoring the camera by the front gate. Jerry had just pulled up, so she rushed a quick explanation as she prepared to go outside.

"That was Kathy and Mark. Mark wants to come help and thinks he can be here in two hours. Hopefully, he'll get here before things get too rough."

Honk! Honk! Came the impatient noise from Jerry's car.

"It'll be good to have Mark if he can get here in time. Right now, we need to deal with Jerry before he makes too much racket," said Mac.

Alex opened the door, careful not to let himself be seen. DD stepped out, and Alex closed the door behind her. She headed for the gate and waved at Jerry as she approached. Her right hand fished a ring of keys from her pocket. She also noticed that the sun was starting to wane and realized the evening was drawing near. She tried to behave as normally as possible.

Inside the office, Mac positioned himself just behind the door and held a piece of rope about 2-foot-long. The ends of the rope were coiled firmly around each hand. Alex stood around the corner, out of sight, with an 18-inch-long piece of steel rebar.

"Hey Jerry, come on in," DD said, opening the gate. As he pulled through, she continued, "Just pull up next to the office; this shouldn't take too long."

"Alright, will do."

Jerry thought it was odd that she locked the gate behind him. Still, he just wanted to get this payroll thing settled and get out of here. He stepped out of the car as she approached. She motioned for him to take the lead up the walkway, so he stepped in front of her and headed for the office.

"It should be unlocked. I'm the only one here. Alex had to go out of town unexpectedly," she explained, hoping he would buy the ruse.

Jerry reached for the door and stepped in. The first thing he noticed was the strong smell of bleach. He was a little startled when, out of the corner of his eye, he noticed DD closing the door from the outside. He wondered why she wasn't coming in. Before he could fully process his thought, he felt an excruciating gagging sensation.

Gasping for air, he realized something was around his neck, and someone was behind him. He felt helpless, and he believed that he was going to die. He thrashed wildly. He felt the blow to his stomach and expelled any remaining air he had. The pain and lack of oxygen made him crumple to the floor. Now, he was reaching wildly with his hands, hoping to find something with which to fight back.

"Calm down, pendejo!" said a voice next to his ear. "If you calm down, my friend will let you breathe." The promise of being allowed to breathe was enough to get him to resist his instincts and stop fighting. As he relaxed, Mac loosened his grip enough to let him get some air but kept enough control to ensure that he was unwilling to fight back. Jerry gagged and coughed. It took him a full minute to collect himself. He looked up, still breathing heavily, and saw Alejandro standing over him with a rusty bar of steel.

"Alex... What the hell, man?" Alex looked at Mac to make sure he still had a tight grip. Mac nodded that he did. Alex, with a quick and sudden move, smacked Jerry across the face with the rebar. The strike landed with a *thwack*, and Jerry's body lurched to the side. Mac had to struggle to hang on to him. It was difficult to hold him up now because he was half limp. Alex grabbed him by the hair and lifted his face to look at him. The red welp was growing. Alex couldn't help thinking that it was nearly the same wound Juan had gotten during his first assault. Alex wondered if he had broken Jerry's cheekbone or loosened any of his teeth. Jerry was struggling to regain focus, and his eyes were darting to and fro.

Alex got in his face and began to speak.

"You sorry snitch. You led those thugs to my best friend! You sold out Juan, you greedy little turd!"
It was the first time Jerry could think clearly enough to realize what was going on. Somehow, Alex had figured out that he had let the suited man know where Juan was.

"I didn't know they would hurt him, man. I didn't know he'd die. Please don't hurt me. I'm so sorry," he pleaded with Alex.

Mac was ready to get this man secured. He looked at Alex and made eye contact. He nodded toward the chair they had placed in the center of the room. Earlier, they had made sure the blinds were closed so that no one could be a witness to what they were doing. It was an extra measure, really. Most people wouldn't be able to see past the gate. Still, having the blinds closed made them feel better.

"My friend here is going to stand you up. Once you're up, come sit in this chair," he said, pointing.

Mac jerked Jerry up with such force that his neck popped, and he started to gag again. He staggered toward the chair with this man controlling his direction with the rope like a set of reins. Once seated, Alex grabbed the zip ties and secured his legs to the chair, then zip tied his arms together behind him. Finally, mercifully, the rope came off his neck.

An unfamiliar man stepped in front of him.

"So, Alex, this is the piece of trash that sold out Juan?"

"Yeah, man."

"Look at me, you worm!"

Jerry strained to lift his head to try to make eye contact.

"I got my ass kicked because of you. I watched your friend die. Tell me one thing, you greedy bastard... How much did you make?"

Jerry's neck still hurt. His face was throbbing, and he was coming to realize that bones in his face were likely broken. With his tongue, he felt his teeth and concluded that several were loose. The vile, iron taste of blood was making him gag, so he spat on the floor to clear his mouth. When some of the blood landed on Alex's boot, he was enraged. He reacted with another sharp *thwack* to his knee, and Jerry let out a yelp.

"Mister... I asked you a question. How much!?"

Blood was still filling Jerry's mouth. He had to spit again. He turned his head this time and made sure he didn't get any on Mac or Alex. The next bolus of saliva and blood splatted on the floor. Once his mouth was clear, he was able to muster a response.

"Five hundred and seven fifty... Five for the first day and the second was seven fifty. Alex, I'm so sorry. I didn't know they would hurt him. I was just trying to make a few bucks," Jerry said with blood streaming down his chin.

"Alex, let me get this straight," began Mac. "This piece of trash sold your lifelong friend out for twelve hundred and fifty bucks?"

"Yeah, man. That's what it works out to."

"Hey, piss ant? What do you think we should do to you?"

"Man, just let me go. I'll never do it again. I promise!"

"Not good enough," said Alex.

It occurred to Jerry that they just might kill him. He began to beg.

"Please, Alex. I'll do anything you want. Please don't kill me!"

Mac kept an intentionally fierce look about himself, but this man was already starting to wither under the pressure. Possibly, he would cooperate enough so they wouldn't have to manhandle him for the next part of their plan.

Alex looked at Jerry and asked demandingly, "Anything!?"

"Yes! Anything! Just promise you won't kill me." Alex and Mac looked at one another. Their initial assault had gotten the punk in the state of mind they wanted. Jerry would do whatever they asked. They both knew the next step, and at a single word from Mac, they continued.

"Bait?"

Alex nodded and stepped out of the room. Jerry was confused and couldn't help but question Mac.

"Bait? What the hell does that mean?"

"You'll see in a minute."

When Alex returned with the suit, Mac couldn't help but notice that the bloodstains were nearly gone, and the holes were sewn up. From across the room, the suit looked pretty good. Up close, you could see the stitching and dark stains where the blood had been.

"DD did a great job getting the suit ready," Mac commented.

Jerry was totally confused. He didn't understand why Alex would've brought a suit into the room. He listened as the conversation between Alex and Mac continued.

"What do you mean, DD? I did this. I sewed the holes."

Mac shrugged his shoulders as if he was pleading for his own innocence, "Sorry, man. I just assumed it was DD. I didn't mean to make you mad."

"All good, man. No harm, no foul. But dude, just know that I can sew. My mom made me learn."

"How about the shirt?"

"I couldn't get the blood out, so I grabbed one out of my closet. It should fit well enough to confuse 'em."

Jerry was lost in this conversation, but he kept his mouth shut because he didn't want to provoke either of them. He felt a Pavlovian chill creep down his spine as Mac stepped behind him. Alex walked in front of him and held up the suit.

"Jerry, since you're so willing to do anything we ask, my friend and I have a small favor. We're gonna cut you loose and have you put this suit on," he said, extending it towards him.

Jerry was still lost, so he asked the obvious question, "Why?"

"We thought it fitting that, since you led Juan to his death, you wouldn't mind being the bait that we use to catch his killers."

Jerry understood his situation and began to protest.

"Please don't make me do it! They'll kill me!"

From behind him came Mac's firm voice, "We could kill you now."

The next sound Jerry heard stole his last bit of fight. It was the obvious *click* of a hammer being pulled back on a gun.

Mac continued, "In case you're wondering, it's a .45," he said, as he pressed the barrel of the gun against the back of Jerry's head.

"Okay... Okay... I'll do it," and with that, he obediently surrendered to their will.

Alex laid the suit on the counter and pulled a pair of snips from his pocket. In a matter of moments, Jerry's hands and legs were free. From that point, Mac never flinched with his pistol aimed at Jerry's center mass. Over the next ten minutes, he stripped down and redressed in the suit. He was close to being finished, but his hands were trembling as he struggled to tie his tie. Alex eventually had to help him.

"Okay, now what?" asked Jerry.

It was Mac that gave the instructions.

"Grab the chair you were sitting in. We're heading out the back door of the office and going to the workshop."

Jerry nodded and grabbed his chair. Alex opened the door and held it for Jerry and Mac. They crossed the space between the office and the workshop rather quickly.

When the workshop door was opened, Jerry's eyes widened as he took in the medieval site.

"Gentlemen, I see you've brought me a worm to bait our hook," said DD.

"What the fu..."

Whack!

Alex hit him across his back with the steel again before he could finish. For a moment, he couldn't breathe. When he gathered himself, he decided not to speak. He simply looked around the room. Some of the workbenches had been pushed back against the walls. They had cleared a space about twenty feet in diameter in the center of the room for their plan. DD stood in the middle of the cleared-out space. She was holding a chain that extended up to the ceiling and attached to a pulley system. The mechanics used it quite often because the electric motor made it easy to lift several tons. On the end of the chain was a large, steel hook.

"Take your chair over to her and sit down," commanded Mac.

He did as he was instructed. Seconds later, he could feel his legs and wrists being strapped to the chair by Alex. Alex cinched the zip ties much tighter this time. With that completed, Mac lowered his .45, and DD continued by hooking the chain on to the back of the chair. Alex simply smiled as he walked over to the control panel on the wall. He pressed the "up" button with his thumb. Once the slack on the chain had been taken up, the chair started to slowly rise into the air.

"Mac, you were right," said DD.

"What's that?"

"He does look like bait dangling from a fishing line."

Jerry didn't think any of this was funny.

"You guys are crazy. They're going to kill me."

"Probably," said Mac.

"You were part of getting Juan killed. I've got no pity for you," said DD with an icy coldness.

"Hey, Alex, bring him down for a sec. I forgot the gag and hood," said Mac.

"No problem," Alex said, pressing the down button.

When he was low enough, Mac tried to put a gag in his mouth. It was difficult because Jerry was swearing and thrashing his head about. Mac unholstered his .45 and smacked him across his face. The blow landed in the same place as before, and Jerry could feel the bones give way under the swollen flesh of his cheek. The resistance stopped, and both the gag and hood were secured in mere seconds.

"Ok, raise him back up."

Dangling from the chair, Jerry could feel the zip ties digging into his wrists and legs. Excruciatingly, the ties strained to hold his rag doll carcass in the chair. With his head covered and his mouth gagged, his protests didn't amount to much. Like a worm on the end of a hook, he fought and tried to wriggle. All his efforts were useless, and in the end, he just started to whimper. The three stood and listened to him hopelessly sob.

"Big bait for a big fish," said Mac.

CHAPTER 21

Arrows to the Heart

Twang....... thunk.

Stacy felt a little awkward being in a place like this in her work clothes. She thought she was way overdressed in her skirt and heels. Her experience in sporting goods stores was limited to purchasing running shoes or finding the next cute exercise outfit. She had never been in the hunting section of the store. She was amazed to see the selection of hunting equipment to include camouflage, guns, ammo and archery equipment. She watched with fascination as Eli put another arrow on his string. When he drew the arrow back, she noticed the muscles in his forearms, shoulders and back get taut. She was amazed at how strong this gentle giant was.

Twang....... thunk.

She was astonished at the two distinct sounds: one as the arrow came off the bow and the other as it hit the target.

He lowered the bow and turned to her, "Would you like to give it a shot?"

Although she was intrigued and might like to try it in the future, she declined.

"Um... I'd like to, but I don't feel dressed for the occasion," she said, knowing her excuse wouldn't fly.

"I love archery. It makes me concentrate to the point that I have to block the entire world out. For me, it's a way to relieve stress."

"Stress therapy? I've been stressed for months. You really think it'd help?"
Eli shrugged his shoulders.

"Only one way to find out," he said with a grin, extending the bow towards her.

He began by showing her how to stand, draw the bow, aim and release the arrows smoothly. Her initial attempts missed the target completely. She thought shooting the bow might hurt. Once she had taken a few shots, however, she realized she would be okay and started to settle down. After some coaching, she started to get closer to the target. The thing that made her improve the most was when she stopped being startled at the release. Eventually, she could keep her eyes open during the shot.

Eli teased her lightheartedly about having her eyes closed. They laughed, and she really started to enjoy the experience. After about twenty minutes, her arms were aching and sore from drawing the bow. She wanted to take one more shot. She put the arrow on the string and drew back. She was trembling with fatigue while she was trying to hold it steady. Her muscles were burning.

Steady..., she thought.

Twang....... thunk.

"Nice shot! Just a few inches away from the bull's eye."

"Whew! That was more fun than I thought it would be," she said, shaking out her arms. "I'm gonna be sore tomorrow."

Eli was happy to see her smile. He felt that, in some way, he had brought some joy into her dark world. He knew the afternoon had not been wasted.

"Glad you liked it."

"Liked it?! It's the most fun I've had in years."

"That makes me happy. I hope you've had a good afternoon," he said, looking at his watch.

She started to tease him playfully, "The last hour's been great. The first three hours were so boring! Why didn't we start with this?" Stacy snickered and playfully punched his shoulder.

He laughed and lightly punched her back on the shoulder. They both started giggling like giddy schoolmates.

After a moment, Eli said, "Hey, let me turn this bow in at the counter, then I can get you back to April's Diner to pick up your car."

She protested, "Wait a minute. You're not gonna buy the bow?"

"I wanted to come and test it. I already have one that I use for hunting. This is just the newer model. It was good, but I think I might wait until next season," he explained.

"What about me?"

"What about you?"

"Well, I was thinking that I had so much fun, I could buy one."

Eli was surprised.

"I didn't expect that. I think it's cool, but it's totally up to you."

"Will you come back and coach me some more?" she said, hoping he would say "Yes."

She did want to shoot. She had really enjoyed it. More than that, though, she enjoyed time with this man. Her feelings for him were like a daughter to a father. Deep inside, she knew she was using the bow purchase as leverage to get more of his time.

"I'd be happy to help you," replied Eli.

"Good. It's settled. Help me pick some arrows and find an armguard that fits."

They headed off together to finish their shopping. Stacy couldn't remember the last time she felt this safe.

CHAPTER 22

The Gear Up

Masters was tense as the three large crew cab trucks pulled into a vacant lot three blocks away from Just Plain Rocks. They parked in a row facing the street. They didn't expect any trouble here, but each of them always wanted to be alert. It was like making sure they were always seated facing the door in a restaurant. The drivers got out of their trucks and met in front of the middle truck.

The unknown man spoke first.

"Let's go over the plan one more time. There may be lots of bullets flying, and I don't wanna take any friendly fire."

This man was more rugged than the rest, and Masters knew this man was quite capable. When they met earlier to review the plan, they were introduced for the first time. Rico said his name was "Dead Ted." According to Rico, he had been a collector for the family loan shark since he was a teenager. He had moved up the ranks quickly because of his willingness to do violence whenever asked.

Dead Ted had been witness to a lot of death over the years, much of it by his own brutal hands.

"Masters, this is your show. Hit the highlights one more time," said Rico James.

"Okay, we three are the team leads. Each of us has two men with us. Me and my boys will drive to the front and clear the gate. Ted, you and your guys will head around back and cut through the fence. Do you guys have your bolt cutters?"

Ted nodded.

"All right, my guys have theirs, too," continued Masters. "While I'm getting the gate, you guys can cut through the fence in the back part of the yard. The goal is to converge on the workshop. Rico, once we get to the workshop, we'll make sure it's all clear. Then we'll call for you to come in."

It was Rico's turn to nod.

"The assumption is that these guys will be waiting for us in the workshop with an ambush. We're gonna want all hands to take the building as fast as possible. I expect that will be the most dangerous part."

"How many do we think are going to be in there?" asked Dead Ted.

"Alex is the one who called, but my assumption is that he's going to have help. Best guess is three or four."

"Dick, with nine of us, we should win. But I don't want to call back East and tell them I lost men. That means, even at the workshop, you and your guys are first in," asserted Rico.

"My boys take orders well. We'll be first in. Just make sure you guys are right behind us."

Dead Ted and Rico both nodded. They were both glad it was Masters and his men going in first. There was no telling what kind of trap they were walking into.

"One more thing," Masters said, getting their attention. "If today goes well, I want a piece of the action."

Rico glared at him. He was angry that Masters would try to leverage this moment for his own greed. On the other hand, though, it was the same kind of thing he would've done himself.

Rico replied, "Let's see how the day goes," knowing he didn't have the authority to make any commitments on behalf of the family.

Dead Ted was annoyed at the extra chatter. He looked at his watch and asked, "When do we leave?"

"It's five thirty-five right now. Let's leave at five forty-five. It's only a couple of blocks away, so I figure we'll be there 10 to 12 minutes early. Maybe being early will be an advantage," said Masters.

Dead Ted wasn't buying it. He figured the other guys were already in place. He didn't like this whole set up. He didn't trust Masters, but he was under orders. He was confident in his own skill, and he planned to come out of this alive. In silence, he turned and walked back to his truck.

* * *

From his perch in the loft of the workshop, Alex could see a big portion of the concrete plant he had spent his life building. He looked at the fencing around the compound and was thankful that, a few years back, he had decided to get some privacy slats for his chain-link fence. His hope at the time was that it would deter theft of his equipment. Although you can still see through it, he was hoping for any advantage, and concealment might just help. At four-forty, he broke radio silence.

"DD, Mac, are you guys in place?"

DD was positioned in the office. The front window faced the gate, and below the windowsill was a row of sandbags that had been placed there for her protection. The front door was locked, and the back door was left unlocked. The plan was for her to watch for any movement at the gate. The theory was that anyone coming in would head for the workshop to get Jerry. She and Mac would try to come in behind them and gain the upper hand. Mac had offered her an AR 15 rifle. Her previous experience with the 5.56 round would serve her well. Besides, it would be better if she had to make a shot that was further out. She patted her hip to make sure she had her faithful Crockett.

"I'm ready," she spoke into her radio.

Mac was stationed out in the yard. There were many places he could move to and use for cover. His role was to be a roving threat in the yard in case someone tried to come in from another direction. There were trucks, piles of sand, heavy equipment and even a couple of small pump houses he could hide behind if necessary. In his mind, he was the free safety, making sure no one got past him. His AR 10 was loaded with a thirty-round mag of 7.62x51mm ammo and he had three spare mags stuck in his vest. He felt very comfortable with this weapon in his hands. If things got up close and personal, he always had his .45 in his holster.

"All good here."

"Okay. Remember, the goal is to get them into the workshop. I'll be in here minding the store, and you guys will come in behind them," said Alex.

Mac and DD both radioed back their agreement.

Alejandro was still uncomfortable with his Glock tucked into the back of his pants. He pulled it out and set it on the floor where he intended to lay prone and watch Masters come in. He would keep it close because he had to. He wished this was a bar fight at The Beer Tap. He would have liked that scenario much better. The other thing that bothered him was the relentless whimpering still coming from Jerry. He knew the zip ties must be digging into his flesh by now. He was sure Jerry was both scared and in pain. He started to feel a little sorry for the guy. He looked at his watch one final time and settled in.

CHAPTER 23

Blood Justice

Masters carefully eased the truck up to the gate and commanded his two men to get out and see if they could open it. Both men exited the truck with great caution and anticipation, and both were armed with HK UMP 9mm sub machine guns. The first man kept watch as the second man checked the gate. There was a chain and lock, but they came prepared for that. One man stepped back to the truck, reached in the bed and pulled out a large pair of bolt cutters. As he worked to snap the chain, the first man was hyper-alert scanning for any movement and listening for any sounds. In a few moments, the chain was dispatched and Masters looked over his left shoulder and saw that Rico was waiting down the block. He knew that Dead Ted was in back cutting through the chain-link fence. Masters wanted to make sure he gave Ted enough time to get through the fence, so he paused for about a minute. This delay made his two goons anxious. They were standing out in the open, and they knew they were vulnerable. They kept looking at him, hoping for the green light to move forward.

In the back of the complex, Dead Ted was making short work of the fence. He had purposefully pulled behind one of the small, outlying buildings in hopes that it would give him some cover. They could cut through the fence and get into the yard without anyone seeing them.

Mac was hiding behind a large pile of sand and could hear the chain link fence being cut. He couldn't exactly pinpoint where the sound was coming from, so he moved to another position behind a mixer truck, hoping to get a better view. He wanted to make sure he had eyes on anyone coming in. But the same buildings and equipment that gave him cover could also be leveraged by his enemies.

Alex was able to see the front gate from his post in the loft of the workshop. He had seen the two men and their fierce looking guns, which made him regret his choice of weapon. He wished he had a rifle or something that could stand a chance against their fire power. A wave of fear tried to grip him, but he pushed it away.

From the office, DD saw the men cut the chain on the front gate. They seemed hesitant to enter.

Why are they just standing there? Her stress level increased, but she resolved to stick with the plan. *Let them walk right past the office and get behind them when they enter the workshop,* she thought. She looked at the back door and felt confident she could slip in quietly behind them.

Mark was in his truck navigating rush-hour traffic on the opposite side of town. He was trying to hurry and, at the same time, avoid being pulled over for speeding. He wanted to know how things were going, but he didn't want to call his friends for fear that a ring from a cell phone might give away their position. He was trying to think of the best way to approach the scene. Coming in the front gate would expose him too much. He would have to circle the property in hopes of finding a less conspicuous entrance.

"Hey, boss."

"Yeah, what?"

"We're sittin' ducks here. We gotta get movin'."

"They should be in by now," Masters said, referring to Ted's team. "One of you get the gate; the other can walk beside the truck."

Depending on where Alex and his folks were, having his men walk next to the truck might offer a little protection. He secretly hoped that Alex had lost his nerve, and this would be easier than expected. In the meantime, he and his men would still have to cross this open space to the warehouse. They felt entirely too vulnerable out in the open.

Mac was still trying to figure out where the sounds were coming from. It was alarming to him, because now it seemed like the noises were coming from two different directions. He found a place behind some cinderblocks where he could see much of the yard. He scanned for any kind of movement. He noticed the sky was pale now and realized it would soon be dark. With the sounds coming from multiple directions, it was almost overwhelming.

"What were we thinking? We need more help. I just can't see everywhere I need to see," he mumbled.

Slowly and steadily, Masters and his men moved across the open area. As they got to the workshop, he was relieved and still hopeful that no one was around.

"Hey, guys, maybe no one's home, but I still don't want to go into the workshop without someone watching our backs. I'm gonna call Rico and tell him to come on in. You guys hunker down and keep your eyes open. We'll cover Rico as he comes through the gate."
The men now had their backs against the workshop and were facing out towards the open space. They still felt vulnerable because they had no real cover, but at least, with a wall at their backs, it was an improvement.

With the men against the wall beneath him, it was difficult for Alex to see them from his loft. He was wondering how he would get a good angle on them when he needed to take a shot. He was trying to be quiet and get into a better position.

Masters picked up his walkie-talkie and began to speak, "We're in front of the workshop. So far, we haven't seen anyone. You're clear to come on in."

"Copy."

From her window in the office, DD had watched Masters cross the lot. The plan was for her to get behind them, but she didn't understand why they were still standing outside the building with their guns out. She couldn't walk out the back door now because they would see her, and she would lose her advantage. She stayed in place, hoping for a better opportunity.

Rico eased his truck down the street and turned slowly into the entrance. He pulled past the gate and was happy to see that Masters had his men covering him. He, too, was hoping the other guys lost their nerve. He was wanting an easy win today.

"When we get past the gate, hop out and close it," he said to one of his men.

When DD saw a second truck come in, it made her gasp.

"That makes six," she said out loud.

When the truck passed the gate, a man climbed out and quickly closed it. There was no way to secure it with the broken chain, but to a casual observer, it would appear locked.

The plan was looking more and more hopeless. DD began to think that catching these guys out in the open may be the best play. They were vulnerable now. She wanted to change the plan but was concerned about radio traffic. She looked for a point of reference. There was a flagpole three-quarters of the way through the lot. She figured since they closed the gate behind them, no one else was coming. She pulled out her phone and started to text. She was hoping the guys had their phones on mute as they had all agreed to earlier in the day.

Simultaneously, both men felt their phones vibrate. They quietly pulled out their phones and checked the message from DD. *Flagpole*

Mac couldn't see anyone. His frustration and stress level were rising. He heard an occasional sound but wondered if he was hearing things. His eyes were darting back and forth looking for something, anything...

The man who closed the gate had not gotten back into the truck. DD now moved to the back window of the office. She could see Masters' men watching and waiting as Rico approached.

Masters thought all had gone well so far. He was beginning to get comfortable knowing Rico and his men were a few steps away. His supposition had always been that the workshop would be the most dangerous place. If they were waiting for him, it would be in there. His mind began to move forward, thinking about how they would get in the building without getting killed.

From a small corner of the office, DD quietly and carefully raised the AR. She began to track the man walking beside the truck with her scope.

Alex had been watching these events unfold. He was trying to get a good angle on the men beneath him. Eventually, he had to stand and point his pistol downward while trying to remain hidden. He knew that when they passed the flagpole, the shooting would start. He wanted to be ready with his target when it happened. He awkwardly aimed his Glock at the man below and to his left.

As the man passed the pole, DD calmly and smoothly squeezed her trigger.

Crack!

The man fell to the ground. When Alex heard the first report, he squeezed his first round off as well.

Boom!

Another man dropped. Dazed and confused, Masters saw his man go down. He was in the open and taking fire. He and his second man darted behind his truck. Rico had already stopped his truck. He and his remaining man climbed out the passenger side, scrambling for cover behind the vehicle.

Neither Alex nor DD could get an angle for another shot. They both watched the men get to the opposite side of their vehicles for cover. Now, it was a waiting game. They had to come out eventually. They trained their guns on the trucks, waiting to see movement.

Mac heard the shots. He hoped the plan was working.

Pew! Pew!

Two shots landed next to him as he instinctively ducked his head. He stooped down and looked for a place to retreat. He saw a cinderblock wall about four feet high that had a right angle. It would give him cover on two sides. He made a dash for it and tripped as he got near. He put his hands out to catch himself, but he planted his face in the dirt.

Pew!

Another shot ricocheted passed him as he rolled behind the cinderblock wall.

He could hear footsteps in the gravel. He raised his weapon to prepare for the next assault. A man ran around the corner and took aim.

Boom!

The man dropped dead twelve feet in front of him. Mac had squeezed his trigger first.

Behind their trucks, Rico and Masters were debating on what to do next. They realized that the shots came from high in the workshop and from the office. After some intense arguing, they decided that they would all have to run at the same time in order to survive. One person making a break for it wouldn't stand a chance. They decided that, if everyone ran, it might be overwhelming enough for some of them to get through.

Rico grabbed his man by the shoulder and said, "We have to get to that office! You run for the front door, and I'll run for the back. Maybe one of us will get lucky." He could see his man was scared but willing.

"Masters," he said, getting Dick's attention. "When we run for the office, you guys run for the warehouse."

"But it's a trap!"

"Oh Hell! In case you haven't noticed, we're already trapped!"

Masters knew Rico was right. He nodded towards his man, letting him know they would be doing what Rico commanded.

Mac continued to take fire. It soon became clear that it was coming from two different directions, and they were adjusting their positions. He knew if he stayed, they would simply close in on him from opposite angles and have the upper hand. Mac eyed a cinderblock pumphouse 20 yards away. If he could get in there, he would at least have walls on four sides.

Back out front, Rico gave the signal, and all four men started to run. Masters and his man were firing at the loft, while Rico and his man were shooting at the office.

Alex saw the men running for the door of the warehouse and shooting at his loft. Hastily, he squeezed off a couple of rounds but missed them both. He heard the door downstairs fly open and knew they had just gotten inside.

DD was taken aback that two men were running at her. She tried to aim but hesitated while deciding which one to shoot. Before she knew it, there was a banging on the front door, and she was glad it was locked.

Mac made sure he had a firm grip on his weapon and knelt forward. He bolted out of his hiding place like an Olympic sprinter and ran for the pumphouse. In his mind, it took an eternity. He smashed through the door, landed on the ground and crawled behind some equipment. It didn't take long before he had his weapon up, aiming at the entrance. He intended to shoot anyone who came through.

The pounding on the front door drew DD like a moth to a flame. She was pulled to it and knew that the man banging outside wanted to kill her. It wouldn't be long before he was able to burst in. She raised her rifle and pointed at the center of the door. Two quick pulls of the trigger and she heard a loud *yelp.*

"One down," she said.

She never heard Rico come in the back door.

Whack!

The pain in her back was instant as she stumbled forward. She felt something jerking at her and realized her AR was being wrenched from her hands. She turned around to see a face full of anger and hatred. She reached for Crockett, but she was overwhelmed as she was violently thrown to the floor. The man standing over her kicked Crockett to the side.

Masters started to creep through the aisles of tools and equipment. He and his man had made it into the workshop without injury. This was of little comfort because he believed the real danger was in this very building. As he eased forward, he gulped hard as he saw a hooded man in a suit hanging from a chain.

That's Lance, he thought, but remembered Lance was just the bait.

He waved and got the attention of his thug. He put his finger over his lips so the man would be quiet. Then, he pointed upstairs because that's where the initial shots had come from. The man simply nodded back, and the two headed quietly towards the steps.

Mac was ready to defend his position in the pumphouse when a brick smashed through the window on his right with a loud clatter. He turned to look and saw the brick land on the floor along with the shards of glass. It was too late. When he looked back at the door, Dead Ted already had the drop on him. Ted's red laser site was dancing across Mac's chest. His heart sank as he realized he was done.

In the loft, Alex was watching the top of the stairs. He could hear footsteps approaching. A man's head appeared, and Alex took a shot. He missed as the man stepped backwards down the stairs. Now, Masters and his man knew what side of the room he was on.

"The only way to get this guy down is if one of us can get up there and even the playing field," Masters whispered to his guy. Masters dropped the magazine out of his weapon and put a new one in. He hit the slide release, and it was ready to go. "I'll reach up and start to fire in the direction the shot came from. That should make him take cover, even if only for a second. When I fire, you run up and find something to hide behind. Then you'll do the same for me."
The man nodded and prepared to run. Masters reached up over the corner and began to fire as fast as he could. The man darted up the stairs and found cover, then he started to fire himself. When Masters heard his man shooting,

he, too, sprinted up the stairs and dove for the nearest cover.

When the gunfire started, Alex had retreated behind a steel pillar. It seemed like a good location at the time.

Masters and his man realized there was only a pillar separating them from Alex. They began to move in opposite directions, flanking him.

Mark could hardly sit still as he was trying to navigate the traffic in town. Another red light, and he threw his hands up in exasperation.

"Hey, you, behind the pillar," yelled Masters. "There's nowhere left to run. Give up now, and we may let you live."

Alex was angry at himself for allowing them to get position on him.

What a rookie mistake.

Deep down, he knew the man was right. He didn't have any other options. In the end, discouragement overwhelmed him, and he threw the Glock on the floor. He slowly raised his hands in surrender.

Stacy could see April's Diner up ahead. She had enjoyed her day with Eli but was ready to get back to her car. Suddenly and violently, Eli slammed on the brakes, and her peace was shattered.

"We gotta go," he said, as he made a wheel squealing U-turn.

"What! What's going on?" she demanded.

"Our friends are in trouble. We have to help!"

"What friends!? How do you know!?"

Already in the industrial park, Eli knew it would only take them a couple of minutes to get there.

As DD gathered her wits, she realized that her captor was standing above her in an aggressive and menacing stance.

"You bastard! Who the hell are you?"

"I'm the guy who's going to kill you if you don't shut your mouth," Rico replied, jerking her to her feet.

DD spit in his face. She was rewarded with a hard and painful slap.

"You bitch! You killed two of my men, and now you spit in my face?"

He pushed her over to the desk and slammed her face down hard onto its wooden surface. The force of the impact left her dazed.

Bam!

A fist came crashing across Mac's face. Dead Ted stood, looking down at him sitting on the floor.

"How many are there?" he demanded.

Mac simply shook his head. He wasn't going to say a word. He looked at the door, hoping to escape. He was glad he wasn't tied up, and for a moment he had hope. Then he realized there was a second man standing in the door.

No way I can get past both of them.

Woomphff.

This time, a boot connected with the bottom of his chin. He fell to his side, writhing in pain.

"I said, how many are there?"

Meanwhile, it was starting to get dark, so no one noticed the man, dressed in black, silently slip through the front gate.

Rico felt completely in control. He wondered if the others had made it to the workshop. He hadn't heard from Ted, and he wondered about the rest of his team, as well. His eyes looked down at DD. She was bent over the desk, and he was leaning against her. He had her pinned so she couldn't get up. He felt her squirm beneath him, and it excited him. He leaned over her and put his full weight on her back.

She felt his breath on her neck and hated him for what he was doing. But what he said next made her want to vomit.

"Lady, you got a nice ass. It may even be good enough to put on the market," he growled in her ear.

"You sorry..."

Whack!

Her sentence was cut short by a punch to the side of her face. She could feel the blood start to seep from the corner of her mouth. With everything in her, she loathed this man.

Alex was now on his knees with his hands tied in front of him. They had brought him down from the loft and made him get on the floor in front of Jerry. Jerry was still whimpering under his hood.

It had gotten fully dark now, so Mark turned off his lights as he approached the entrance to Just Plain Rocks. He looked to see if he could make out any activity. He passed the entrance and circled around back.

"Lance, how the hell did you get caught?" said Masters to the hooded man. He considered shooting him now. The man started to make muffled, pleading sounds like he wanted to talk. Masters looked up and saw the chains and pulley and followed the system along until he could see where the control panel was. He pointed so his man would see where it was.

"Over there. The control panel. Let's get him down."

The man walked to the panel and pressed the "down" button. As the chair came in contact with the floor, Jerry was afforded a measure of relief when the zip ties on his arms and legs were no longer holding his body weight.

Still terrified, he waited for what was next. Masters jerked the hood off and was dismayed when he didn't see Lance.

Rico started to caress DD's butt with his hand. He admired its smooth curve and perfect size. He held her down and rubbed his crotch against her. DD wanted to die.

"Who the hell are you?" Masters screamed at Jerry. Muffled attempts to talk followed until Masters took off Jerry's gag.

"Jerry," he said, gasping. "Please don't kill me!" Masters turn his attention to Alex.

"Who the hell is this guy? Where's Lance? I oughtta kill you both right now," he said, as he raised his pistol.

Rico grabbed the top of DD's jeans, and tried to jerk them down.

Damn belt!

For the first time, DD was glad she was face down. She hoped he couldn't get to her belt buckle. But the man was growing more violent, pulling harder and harder on her pants.

The blows Mac was taking hadn't stopped. Now, he was curled up in a fetal position on the concrete floor of the pumphouse. He knew that if this man didn't shoot him, he would be beaten to death. He determined that, no matter what happened, he wouldn't sell out his friends.

Masters had his gun pointed at Alex's head.

"Where are the audio files? What did you do with Lance?"

Alex hung his head in defeat and waited for Masters to pull the trigger.

Rico continued to hold DD down with one hand as he made progress with her jeans. Another tug or two and her backside was exposed completely.

"Ah, what an ass," he said, slapping it hard. *Smack!* Tears filled her eyes. She had lost all resolve.

Thwack!

The man that had been with Ted fell dead in the doorway of the pumphouse. Dead Ted turned to see his deceased companion lying in the dark doorway. He slowly started to move to the door. He didn't know who was out there. Now it was his turn to be scared. He stepped forward cautiously with his gun pointing at the entrance. He was so worried about the door that he didn't realize he had gotten tunnel vision.

Mark silently moved from the front of the building to the side window that was already broken from the brick earlier. He raised his weapon and took aim. He moved his finger to the trigger and started to squeeze.

Mac had been watching his assailant's reaction to the dead man in the door. He saw his opening and quietly stood. He lunged forward and threw his arm around the man's throat from behind. Mark saw the commotion and took his finger off his trigger. Ted dropped his gun and started to grasp at the arm around his throat. It felt like a python. He couldn't get any air and started to panic. He flailed about, alternately pulling down on the arm and reaching for anything he might get hold of. He started to stagger, but Mac held tight. With every move the man made, he was able to squeeze tighter and tighter. He positioned himself where he could use his other arm to force his neck forward, deeper into the vice. For Ted, things started to go dark. He fell backwards to the ground and continued to pull at Mac's arm, but his hold was relentless. Eventually, Ted's resistance stopped. It was in his death that he truly lived up to his name. For a brief while, there was silence as Mac clung to Ted in the darkness.

"Mac, you ok?" came Mark's voice in a whisper. Mac was still hurting from the assault his body had taken. He pulled himself to his feet.

"Yeah, I'm good," he said, staggering out of the building. "I'm so glad to see you."

Back in the workshop, there was a sudden, CRACK! Masters' thug hit the floor, and a pool of blood started to form around his body. Alex, Masters and Jerry were all bewildered. Masters looked dreadfully into the dark spaces of the room to see where the threat was coming from. Alex could see that Masters was distracted and, although his hands were tied in front of him, he was able to contort enough to get to his boot. He grabbed his knife and held it in both hands that were still bound together. Fear gripped Masters as he struggled to search out the dark. He knew someone had killed his man, and he was likely next. He searched the shadows, terrified of what he might find. Alex leaped from his kneeling position and plunged the knife down with all his might into Masters' back. Masters cried out in pain and fell forward. He crashed to the concrete floor, face first. He was grabbing over his shoulder and behind his back, desperately trying to get the attack to stop, but Alex stayed on his back and continued to stab him. Over and over, he brought the blade down with a penetrating fury. Finally, Masters stopped thrashing, and Alex knew it was over.

Out of the shadows emerged a man dressed in black. Alex recognized him immediately.

"Lenny! Thank God you're here."

A moment later, Lenny had freed Alex.

Mark and Mac looked in the window and saw Alex and Lenny. There didn't seem to be any danger.

"Alex, it's Mac. We're coming in. Don't shoot."

"It's clear, come on in."

Mac and Mark were stunned as they evaluated the grizzly scene. Blood was everywhere. Alex, himself, was covered in the red, sticky mess. In the midst of it all, they were happy to see each other alive. Alex was pleased to see that Mark had arrived, as well. In a few, quick moments, they had all acknowledged one another.

"What are we going to do with him?" Mac said, motioning to Jerry.

"Let's find out about DD and deal with him later," said Alex.
They all agreed that DD was the priority. Jerry was glad he wasn't hanging from the chair anymore. His arms and legs were in so much pain he just sat there whimpering.

DD's terror increased as she heard the zipper on Rico's pants. Her hope had abandoned her.
Boom! Crash!
Eli had used his body as a battering ram. He hit the front door with all his might and knocked it off its hinges. Both the door and Eli came crashing to the floor. Rico was stunned and looked over his shoulder. Animalistically, he refused to let go of his prey and kept DD pinned down. Stacy stepped through the door, bow drawn.

"Never again, you son of a bitch!"
She aimed for the middle of his back and let the arrow fly. *Twang....... thunk.*
It tore through the flesh of his right butt cheek and he cried out in pain. Rico loosened his hold enough for DD to break loose. She threw him off and spun around. In a flash, she had her pants up. Rico fell to the floor, grabbing

for the arrow that was in his butt. DD and Stacy impulsively pounced on him. They were striking every place they could. Rico was swearing and flailing wildly against the onslaught of punches and kicks. DD could feel someone pulling her off. She started to fight the hands grabbing her until she realized it was Alex and Mac. Stacy felt a mighty arm encircle her waist and lift her up. She recognized that it was Eli. As the women were pulled off, Rico looked up, bewildered. He was face to face with Mark and Lenny's guns. When he began to protest, Mark took the butt of his gun and smashed him in the mouth. He still tried to yell at the group that had assembled.

"You don't know what you've done. Do you know who I am?"

Whack!

Another blow from Mark.

They were stunned when Eli began to speak. He held Rico's gaze and declared.

"You have brought wickedness to this city. Judgement is reckoned to you this very night!"

DD was the only one who moved. She stepped over and picked up Crockett from the floor. Without a word, she walked over to Rico, put the barrel to his forehead and squeezed the trigger. Blood splattered across the front of the desk. The sound of the *boom* was deafening. It seemed eternal.

"It...Is...Completed," bellowed Eli.

The whole room grew quiet in a bittersweet relief. One by one, they realized that the ordeal was over.

Mac looked over at Alex and asked, "And what about Jerry?"

"Mercy," Alex replied.

Instinctively, everyone looked to Eli to for his approval.

He nodded.

CHAPTER 24

Closure

The sun was coming up, and the air felt cool and crisp. Mac had parked beneath the sign that said, "Opening Soon: Petrol Max." This is where it had all begun. Alex, Mac and DD were sitting on the tailgate of their JPR work truck. They looked across the lot and saw their dear friend.

Mark looked over from the mixer truck and waved his tattooed arm. The concrete slab he had just poured would be there for many years. It was likely they would all be dead before anyone discovered what was concealed underneath. His next thought was of Kathy. He pulled his phone from his vest and hit speed dial.

"Baby, we did it."
He could hear sobs of joy come through the phone.

Lenny approached the three on the back of the truck. Alex and DD jumped up to give him a hug. Then Mac stuck out his hand, grabbed Lenny's and gave it a hearty shake.

"I'm Mac. I don't guess we've formally met yet."

"My name is Lenny. I'm a captain with the local police department," he said with a grin.

Alex explained, "Lenny's been with us all along. He was our eyes and ears within the PD. Lenny told us from the beginning that there were people on the take in the Department."

The look on Mac's face revealed his epiphany.

"Yeah, our chief was one of them," said Lenny.

"Well, how did you know what was happening? And how are we gonna keep all of this from the rest of the cops," Mac asked.

He had just realized the police may not like what had happened. He was convinced they would all be arrested.

"I knew because the chief told us to stay out of the industrial park after six p.m. That confirmed for me that he was the power player behind it all," explained Lenny.

"You took a big risk coming to the industrial park to help us," said DD.

Lenny looked at her and smiled, "Not really. I walked into the chief's office and called him out on his hypocrisy. It pissed him off, and he started to threaten me. I bluffed him and told him that I had access to phone conversations incriminating him."

"No way!" said Alex, starting to laugh. "You totally punked the Chief!"

"It gets better. I told him that if he didn't resign as chief within ninety days, I would send the audio files to the East Coast mob."

"You did not!" said DD, laughing.

"I did! I really enjoyed having the guy by the balls. He's sold this city out for way too long."

They were busy patting each other on the back and congratulating themselves when another car pulled up.

"Hey, guys," said Stacy, climbing out of her car. "Eli said I might find you here."

Her next move delighted them all. She reached into her car and pulled out a carry tray with six cups of coffee labeled "April's Diner." She carried them over and made sure everyone got one. They called Mark over who was just finishing with Kathy. Soon, they were all sipping coffee, chatting and enjoying each other's company.

When the conversation died down, it was Stacy who spoke first.

"Well, it's almost eight a.m., and I don't have a job to go to."

"What kind of work do you do?" asked Alex.

"I was working for Masters. He paid me like a receptionist, but I did a lot of other things. I kept his books, did payroll and organized his contracting jobs."

"Cool. I need someone with that skill set. Why don't you come work for me?"

Smack!

They all turned and looked as DD hit Alex in the arm.

"Hey, that's my job!" she said in a playful protest.

"Not anymore."

All eyes were on him, and everyone was a little bit confused.

"I've been overworked lately. I've been thinking about either selling JPR or bringing in some help."

He let that sink in. He looked around, and everyone was waiting for him to continue. He loved being the center of their attention.

"DD, Mac, I would like to offer for you two to become partners in Just Plain Rocks!"

"What?" said Mac.

"Are you for real?" asked DD.

"One hundred percent on the level. Of course, I'd keep the majority share," he said, smiling. "But I trust you guys with my life. Why wouldn't I trust you with my company?"

Lenny, Mark and Stacy began cajoling DD and Mac.

"Say yes!"

"Don't give him time to change his mind!"

"Just do it!"

"Tell him 'Yes'!" came their pleas.

DD smiled a huge smile and said, "I accept."

The group went wild and began to look at Mac. Mac stuck out his hand and shook Alex's.

"Absolutely, my friend. I'm happy you asked."
In this moment, everything seemed right with the world.

"A toast...A toast...," said Stacy, holding up her cup.

DD discretely reached over and grabbed Mac's hand. It made her smile when she received a warm squeeze in return.

In unison, they all held up their coffee cups and chimed, "CHEERS!"

* * *

Half a block away, Eli watched them raise their cups. He had grown fond of each of them, but his work was complete. With a tear in his eye, he reached over, put his truck into drive, and pulled anonymously into traffic.

Thank you!

I sincerely appreciate you taking the time to read my first fiction book! It has been an amazing journey that I am continuing. I would love to know what you think of Eli, DD, Mac and Alex. I have future plans and ideas for at least one of them. Please feel free to contact me in any of the following ways:

cbeasley2323@gmail.com
www.brannoncommunication.com
Facebook under BrannComm
Instagram @chrisbeasley23

As you know, readers are the life blood of the book industry. I would love it if you would leave a review for this book on Amazon. I would greatly appreciate your honest feedback.

Thank you, again, for taking the time to read *Executing Justice: Concrete, Crooks and Blood*. Be on the lookout for a new book in the near future!

Sincerely,

Chris Beasley

www.ingramcontent.com/pod-product-compliance
Lightning Source LLC
Chambersburg PA
CBHW050929120626
46552CB00001B/115